FAST RIDE TO BOOT HILL

FAST RIDE TO BOOT HILL

THE LEGEND OF BEN HAWKS

LEE MARTIN

FIVE STAR
A part of Gale, a Cengage Company

GALE
A Cengage Company

Farmington Hills, Mich • San Francisco • New York • Waterville, Maine
Meriden, Conn • Mason, Ohio • Chicago

LIBRARY OF CONGRESS CATALOGING-IN-PUBLICATION DATA

Names: Martin, Lee, 1955– author.
Title: Fast ride to Boot Hill : the legend of Ben Hawks / Lee Martin.
Description: Farmington Hills, Mich. : Five Star, A part of Gale, a Cengage Company, 2019.
Identifiers: LCCN 2019014136 (print) | ISBN 9781432860073 (hardcover : alk. paper)
Subjects: | GSAFD: Western stories.
Classification: LCC PS3563.A724927 F37 2019 (print) | DDC 813/.54—dc23
LC record available at https://lccn.loc.gov/2019014136

First Edition. First Printing: December 2019
Find us on Facebook—https://www.facebook.com/FiveStarCengage
Visit our website—http://www.gale.cengage.com/fivestar
Contact Five Star Publishing at FiveStar@cengage.com

Printed in Mexico
1 2 3 4 5 6 7 23 22 21 20 19

To my beautiful sister, Arlene, all of my wonderful family,
and in the fond memory of our beloved mother,
our rough-riding brothers, and Jim Liontas.

Chapter One

In early summer of 1876, under a cloudy sky, six haunted graves lay north of the rock corrals by a lonely relay station on the vast and rolling red desert of Arizona Territory.

North of the station, white and scarlet cactus flowers quivered in the breeze as a gray coyote, with red flanks and tail tucked in, moved through thorny plants and purple sage on the scent of a small varmint. Far to the south, sheltered among golden blossoms on tall mesquite and paloverde, a half-dozen tan and white spotted pronghorn antelopes cowered with their young, their scent lost in the whistling gusts and whirling dust.

Just north of the main building and west of the hay barn and rock corrals, a large equipment building stood with a side door swinging in the wind.

From the distant southeast, an oncoming rider appeared as a dot on the prairie.

On the station's covered porch, the middle-aged manager, Jed Rhyder, and his Navajo wife looked toward the distant rider approaching. "It could be him," Jed told her.

Silent, she wiped her hands on her white apron. She was younger than Jed, her black hair a sharp contrast to his gray. She had a pretty face and wore a red blouse and skirt she herself had made. Jed's buckskin jacket was likewise the work of her hands. He felt grateful for it, and for her, as he watched the solitary figure on horseback draw closer.

"This will be tough," he muttered, tugging first at his hat and then at the chin strap. Nervous fingers stroked his thin mustache. "I couldn't put that one thing in the letter. But he has a right to know."

The oncoming rider moved through sage and high brush, startling the pronghorns. They sprang to life and danced across the prairie with amazing speed, only to quickly disappear in denser stands of paloverde. High in the darkening sky, a red-tailed hawk, belly white with a black band, hovered silently as if pinned to the clouds. Abruptly, it swept eastward on the trail of a black-tailed jackrabbit, which dived into dark sage and out of sight. The hawk swooped down, then hurled itself back into the sky.

In the station's corral, a dozen horses stood with tails to the wind. Jody, the young wrangler and station hand, fought to close the side door to the barn. A sudden gust of wind blew his hat backward, only the chin strap keeping it on him. He yanked hard on the door and managed to shut it, then headed for the equipment barn to secure its swinging door as well.

Dust and debris spun in the air. All reflected loneliness and desolation in the face of the coming storm. The rider was close enough now to recognize, and Jed wiped his brow with the back of his hand. "So now I have to break his heart."

Jed's wife touched his sleeve as if in silent understanding; she returned inside the station as the gusts grew stronger. Jed tightened his chin strap and watched the visitor ride around the barn to the north side of the corrals where the graves were.

Jed spat tobacco juice away from the wind. He walked uneasily down the station steps and made his way to the grave site, reaching it as the stranger dismounted from his sorrel gelding.

Each grave bore a crude wooden cross on which a name was carved. On the nearest one, a blue hair ribbon dangled over the name *Lora Bedloe*.

The stranger stood quiet, gazing at the markers.

Jed approached cautiously and spoke over the noise of the wind. "You must be Ben Hawks."

The young Texas Ranger nodded and moved closer to the graves. Wearing a black leather vest, a single-action Army Colt at his right hip, and a wide-brimmed hat, he stood so tense he could have been a statue. His red bandanna flapped in the wind, but the hat stayed put as if it dared not blow away. Clean-shaven and handsome, Hawks turned toward Jed, revealing dark fury in his ice-blue eyes.

Jed drummed up his courage but had trouble coming up with the right words. What he had to say would be painful to any man who had lost a sweetheart to violence. "I'm sorry, son. Nearest we could figure, there was a running battle in the pass. A horse went down. The coach hit some rocks and busted free of the hitch, and went rolling downhill. Everyone got killed."

Jed didn't say he felt none of them could rest in peace after what happened.

He wiped his mouth with the back of his hand. He also couldn't bring himself to say the rest of it, to bring this man any more agony.

Ben slowly turned and moved toward his sorrel gelding. It carried his bedroll, possible sack, and saddle bags. A Winchester repeater rested in the scabbard. The young man's heavy silence made Jed wince, but he walked alongside him and forced himself to continue.

"Boss said your lady there, she worked for the express company down in El Paso and was on a pass to visit a cousin in California." Jed waited, but received no response. Hawks stood silent like a statue in the driving wind.

He couldn't say the one thing that could get him shot. "What she still had on her, we sent off to Texas. The letter she'd written you but hadn't mailed as yet, and the locket with both of you in it. She sure was pretty. And all that dark brown hair."

Hawks' mouth tightened. Unnerved, Jed held onto his hat. "Two of the gang got killed in the fight. Their faces were right there on *Wanted* posters. It was Avery's bunch, all right."

Hawks tightened the cinch on his saddle.

"Biggest shipment ever. Headed for Tucson and California. A lot of it was newly minted gold coin. Packs of new currency. All a big secret. Even we was never told. But somebody was, that's for sure."

Slowly, the young ranger stroked his mount's shoulder.

"Are you going after Avery?" Jed asked.

Hawks nodded as he swung into the saddle.

Jed drew back. "Good luck, son."

Still without a word, Ben Hawks reined about and rode away, headed back toward the rough, painted hills in the southeast. Beyond them, Jed knew, lay the trail to Texas.

He spat tobacco juice and watched it spin away from him in the wind. Days like this, he felt like he'd lived through a hundred years of experience in half the time.

Jody came up behind him. The pink-faced wrangler's jacket flapped around him and he hung on to his hat as he stared after the distant rider.

Jed wiped his mouth with the back of his hand again. "That was hard."

"What did he say?"

"Not a word."

"Scary."

"You have no idea."

"Did you tell him the rest of it?"

"No, I was plumb scared he'd shoot me. And I just couldn't load that on top of whatever guilt he's gonna carry with him. 'Count of our boss said as how it was Hawks got her the express job in the first place."

Jody grabbed his hat as it flew up; he clamped it back on his head. The two of them leaned into the wind, still watching Ben Hawks became a shadow on the distant prairie. After a while, Jed shook his head. "All I could get out was how pretty she looked when I was saying about the locket."

"I still can't figure why it was only her and not the men." They walked toward the station as rain began to fall.

"I don't know the why of it," Jed grunted. "But I think Avery had a run-in with the rangers in Texas some time back, so they could have tangled with Hawks. And maybe if they knew about the shipment, they also found out his fiancée was on board. So they could have done it just to torment Hawks. Send him a message."

"What do you think he'll do now?"

"All I can say is, if I was Brian Avery, I'd be shaking in my boots."

Another gust drove rain into their faces, and Jody nearly lost his hat for the fourth time. "But nobody knows what Avery looks like."

"I figure Ben Hawks'll kill him a hundred times before he gets the right one."

"And then what?"

"Only the good Lord knows the answer."

CHAPTER TWO

In early fall of 1879, Ben Hawks, no longer a Texas Ranger, packing twin holsters, and just turned thirty, rode north with a friend on the red and gold prairie in western New Mexico Territory.

A letter had been waiting for him at a ranger station in Texas when he stopped in to see his old comrades. A letter from a deputy US marshal in Carmody. Just a few lines saying he had some news about the '76 stage robbery. What Ben read made him want to do as the songs claimed he did and ride the night sky to get there as fast as he could, but he knew that wasn't a wise idea. Traveling with his friend Luke helped slow him down long enough to plan, at least a little.

Luke Ramsey, an old-timer who'd done scouting for the army, had been good if mostly silent company. Middle-aged, with receding gray hair, Luke looked weary, as if he should have retired a long time back. His buckskin jacket tied behind the cantle of his saddle, he rode cooler in his blue army shirt. His sweat-stained hat had seen better days.

They took a noon break in the shade of a large pinyon pine, its nuts already open. Nearby lay a water hole, nearly dry but with enough left to refresh their mounts. Paloverde and thorny cactus surrounded them, and the stench of yellow marigolds mingled with the pungent smell of purple sage. Dark mountains rose to the west and over in the east.

Luke's grumpy bay nipped at Ben's peaceful chestnut gelding. The chestnut ignored the aggravation and kept cropping the sparse grass, white tail switching back and forth.

"My Shorty is jealous of your gelding," Luke said. Ben managed a grin, but his heart wasn't in it.

They shared jerky and hardtack while sipping from their canteens.

"All this way and you never said why you quit the army," Ben said after a time.

"I told you, I was going home to my wife."

"You been in Texas a mighty long time and never spoke of her."

"Well, I made trips to see her, and the last one was a doozy."

"You might want to get a new hat," Ben suggested as he capped his canteen. He liked Luke but never could get a fix on him. That he had a wife added to the mystery of the man's life.

"She don't care about my hat," Luke said.

"So she'll just be glad to see you?"

"You could say that," Luke grunted, and then looked embarrassed and proud both at once. "She's gonna have another kid."

Ben, startled, couldn't respond. Luke didn't look like a daddy, not after so much time trailing Apaches for the army. He always looked grumpy, dirty, and what Ben thought of as old.

"I know," Luke said with a grin. "But remember, son, just because the roof is gray don't mean there ain't no fire in the furnace."

Ben held back his smile. "Okay, so how many does this make?"

"Ten."

"*Ten?*"

The older man laughed, likely at the look on Ben's face. "We got nine boys, so I'm hoping we get a girl this time."

Ben nearly collapsed in amazement. "God bless you."

"Time I stayed home for good," Luke said. "I didn't know

how tired I was till I got to trailing with you."

"You're tired? What about your wife?"

Luke had another good laugh, but Ben remained astounded. "I've seen how slow you get around, Luke. I can't figure how you ended up with ten kids."

Luke grinned. "All it takes is a little incentive."

"You're a lucky man."

"Well, maybe I ain't said nothing about what you been doing all over the frontier in every direction, but if you'd have stopped and got your life back, you could have a couple kids of your own by now."

Ben wiped his brow. He didn't tell Luke he had dreams of seeing Lora alive, when he knew she had died with five other people on that coach. Feigning casualness, he shrugged. "It could be that marshal's letter will lead me to Brian Avery."

"And if it don't?"

"Then maybe you're right. Except I'm not sure I can stop."

Luke gave him a somber look. "You get to Carmody and you don't get no satisfaction, promise me you'll think about what I said."

"Yeah, okay, I will."

Later in the afternoon sun, Luke headed northeast toward the mountains, the Rio Grande, and then on up to Santa Fe. With regret, Ben watched him disappear amid the rocky terrain. Luke had been a loyal friend for years, even though they hadn't ridden together except when they shared a trail with the army, Apaches, and at times with Comanche. Ben always had trouble with the latter, since his mother was a quarter Comanche and often had relatives on the warpath. At home, she conducted her own warpath when he bucked her determination to get him off Avery's trail.

"It's no good," she'd said. "You're wasting your life."

He knew she hadn't liked or trusted Lora, which added to the trouble. Finally, after considerable argument, she had respected Ben's choice to pursue Avery and his gang. Not easily, but it was something.

Ben continued north toward Carmody, which lay near the northwest mountain range. Alone again, he missed Luke's company. The aging scout had given him hope that he could end his lonely trail. Despite Luke's encouragement, he wondered if he would ever get off this haunted trail of vengeance.

After a time he started talking to his horse, just to hear the sound of a human voice. "I reckon you're getting mighty tired of this, Tex, but maybe there's good news waiting at Carmody." He cast an eye to the sky and then northward. "Maybe we can bring it to an end, once and for all." He didn't really believe it. But Luke had forced him to face the fact that he'd wasted the past three years. Having zeroed in on Avery, Ben had looked neither left nor right. Just chased his quarry, determined to avenge Lora, no room in his mind for another woman or children or any kind of settling down.

Could he even love another woman? Lora had been a surprise and overwhelmed him. He found it unlikely any other woman would see a husband in Ben Hawks. Especially with the stories told about him in saloons and around campfires, stories that made clear he wasn't the marrying or settling kind.

As his reputation grew in his search for members of the Avery gang, songs were written to celebrate his deadly hunt. One of them, printed in dime novels, had him riding the sky at night, his pair of well-oiled Army Colts ready for either hand, his every shot faster than sound. Since then, many an upstart gunslinger had challenged him and ended up dead on Boot Hill.

He told himself the good Lord had kept him alive to bring Avery to justice. At the same time, he feared that nothing, not even finding Avery, could remove the knife from his heart.

He shifted his weight in the saddle. "Hold on, Tex, I figure we'll be there in another hour. And maybe it will soon be over." Talking took his mind off the silence on the prairie, but only for a short while. Wherever he rode, there would always be someone with a dime novel praising his exploits, painting him as invincible. The irony of it was, Ben had never wanted anyone to know of him except Avery. But the outlaw and his gang remained elusive. He'd been forced to kill two of Avery's men in a single gunfight down in El Paso, which added to his legend, but he'd learned nothing from the men before they died. The one who lingered a few minutes had insisted Avery was dead.

Ben didn't believe him.

The two dead outlaws made little difference in the numbers. Brian Avery and at least a dozen of his men, every one of them ready to ambush Ben, could be anywhere. He wouldn't know Avery if the man walked up to him on the street in a one-horse town somewhere. The outlaw had a reputation for disguise, and no one was sure exactly what he looked like. But as he continued his long search, Ben wondered if he would soon lose himself.

"Lord, will it never end?" he whispered. The silence of the land gave him too much time to think and remember.

As alone now as a man could be, he felt grateful when a little brown white-breasted wren scolded his passing in its loud, rough voice from somewhere in the waving grass. "Okay, okay," Ben responded. "We're leaving." Now he conversed with birds. He shook his head at what had become of him.

Finally, further north on the brown sweep of the grasslands, his destination came in sight. The little cow town of Carmody, basking in the afternoon sun. In the southern sky, a black buzzard, red head bare and startling, circled gracefully. Wings spread in a V, it soared above the landscape. Ben had spotted the scavenger bird a few times in the past couple of hours.

"There he is again, Tex," he said. Part of him wondered if it was some kind of omen.

As if it had heard, the buzzard swooped beyond the far ridge to the west.

As Ben neared the town, the scenery began to change. Toward the north and west, dark clouds hung over the circling mountains, which rose behind sandstone cliffs streaked with crimson and yellow. Below the cliffs, cattle grazed on rolling hills dotted with dark pinyon pine, scrub oaks, and golden aspens. To the east, he could see another mountain range, less colorful. The only sounds were the creaking of his saddle and his horse's hoofbeats on the hard, dusty ground. The smell of the animal's sweat mingled with the heavy aroma of sagebrush.

Ben made the sign of the cross on his chest. "All right, Tex," he said. "Let's pray this is it."

He rode into Carmody and reined his horse to a halt halfway up the single street, where a few horses stood at the rails near a saloon on the right. Ben saw no one on the boardwalk, only faces at windows. It came as no surprise. He could never figure how they knew he'd arrived, but people always did.

Across the dusty street to his left, an empty wagon with two mules blocked the rail by the office of the deputy US marshal. A creaking windmill loomed beyond the corrals by the livery at the far end of town. After the long, hard trail up from Mesilla, Ben felt dirty and worn and on edge. He turned his weary mount rightward, reining up at the rail in front of the express office, just past the saloon. A two-story hotel stood just ahead, next to a barber shop. He thought of food and rest for himself and his gelding.

And he had no patience for what he heard behind him as he dismounted.

"Hawks, turn around."

Belatedly conscious of faces staring out from inside the

express office, he tugged at his wide-brimmed hat and draped the reins over the hitching rail.

"Hey, Hawks!" The man's voice rang loud in the silent street.

Ben felt cold sweat running between his shoulder blades. His twin Colts hung low and tied down, ready to leap into his hands. He turned slowly, conscious of an old man hurriedly pulling his burros back into the distant livery corral.

In the middle of the dusty street stood a gunman with a silver-studded gun belt. Somewhere in his thirties, probably. His right hand hovered near a low-slung, pearl-handled Colt. Slim, narrow faced, and wide-mouthed, he slowly lifted his left hand and pushed his hat back from his curly brown hair. Putting on a show, he spread his boots and took a stance. A half-crushed yellowish smoke dangled from his pale lips. His brown eyes flashed with arrogance.

"You remember me, Hawks? Four years ago, down in Texas. You shot a friend of mine."

Ben stood silent, watching him.

"I'm the Pecos Kid."

Ben did not respond.

"Hawks, I'm running you out of town."

Ben turned his back. He lifted a stirrup and hooked it over the saddle horn. He began to loosen the cinch, knowing any moment that fool could shoot him in the back, but the man's reflection in the express office window gave enough warning.

Trying to save face, Pecos taunted him. "I know about your woman."

The squeaking of the distant windmill sounded louder in the hush. Face burning, Ben slid his left hand into his horse's white mane and gripped hard, but didn't turn.

Pecos kept after him, sounding annoyed. "Three years ago, wasn't it? Stage holdup."

Despite himself, Ben broke his silence. "Were you there?"

"No, but everyone heard about it."

Ben tried to swallow and could not. He kept his back to the man but knew it couldn't last for long. His horse tossed its head and eyed him. Fury rose within him, and he fought to control it. He hadn't ridden all this way for a gunfight with some fool upstart.

He kept his eye on the man's reflection in the window.

"They say you went plumb loco." Pecos was grinning now. "Quit the Texas Rangers. Been hunting Avery's gang ever since. And killing everyone gets in your way."

Ben stroked Tex's strong neck, then ran a hand down the horse's left foreleg. The gunman snickered and kept at it. "I hear your ma's a quarter Comanche. You must be dirty all over."

Dark with anger, Ben turned very slowly.

Pecos sneered and spoke even louder. "You went and got yourself a fancy reputation. Got songs about you and them bandits along the border. And how you ride across the sky at night. And they call you the fastest draw there ever was. So how about me, Hawks? Think you can beat the Pecos Kid?"

Color rose hot in Ben's face and throat. He moved away from his horse and into the street. Conscious of men watching at windows and doors of nearby frame buildings, Ben paused some twenty feet from Pecos, who snickered again. "Now, Hawks, if you wanna run scared, get out of town. And I won't even laugh."

Silent, Ben stood waiting.

Pecos looked a bit unnerved. He laughed a little shakily, then spat the smoke from his lips, letting it drop to the dirt. "I'm gonna toss a silver dollar in the air. When it hits the ground, we draw."

Ben kept both hands at his sides. He could use either weapon with ease, but his right was his surest. Maybe he could just wing

Pecos, put a stop to this. And maybe learn if Pecos had ridden with Avery.

Pecos' confidence beamed in his face as he took a silver dollar from his vest pocket and held it up. Ben could see it was solid with no hole in the center. He tensed, working his fingers, sweat trickling down his back. There had to be a time when someone was faster than him. He didn't want it to be now, not before he found Avery.

Pecos tossed the coin high in the air and off to the side. The silver glow of it caught the sunlight. Pecos smiled crazy-like, eyes narrowing, lips curling back over his teeth.

Before the coin hit the dirt, Pecos drew whistle fast.

Ben was faster, his Colt leaping into his right hand. He fired as Pecos pulled the trigger. Ben's bullet hit Pecos high in the right shoulder, while the gunman's lead whistled past Ben's neck. The shots echoed in the empty street.

Pecos staggered forward, then stopped. He stared at Ben with his six-gun wavering in his right hand, blood showing high up on his shirt, his eyes wild. He dropped to his knees with a shudder. Still trying to hold his gun, he grabbed at his wound.

Ben saw the crowd gathering along both sides of the street. A young doctor, wearing spectacles and in his shirt sleeves, came forward and knelt next to the wounded Pecos, who cussed angrily. Two men came and helped Pecos to his feet. The doctor stood and walked up the street ahead of them, clearly expecting Pecos and his helpers to follow.

Ben breathed a silent prayer as he holstered his Colt. He turned to calm his gelding, his back to Pecos and the rest. In the window of the express office, he saw Pecos shaking off his helpers, then turning back toward Ben.

He spun around as the wounded Pecos held up his six-gun in both hands and the men around the gunslinger scattered.

Ben moved clear of his horse and pulled his Colt, cocked the hammer back, and fired.

Pecos' bullet whistled past Ben and his horse. His own shot hit Pecos in the chest, dead center.

Pecos doubled up, staggered forward, and crumpled to the ground in a heap. The young doctor came hurrying back, knelt to have a look, then stood and shook his head. The crowd on the boardwalks stood gazing at Ben.

Ben holstered his Colt with a feeling of disgust. He'd been challenged too many times in the last three years. It had grown painful and hindered his every move. The Lord might frown on him for not turning away, yet the challenges kept coming. What was he supposed to do?

"Stop right there," a deep, gruff voice called.

Ben turned to see a stocky man in his late sixties, a circle star on his vest, crossing over toward him from the left side of the street. The lawman's rough, lined face and squinting gray eyes didn't look too friendly. His thick red mustache twitched as he paused a few feet away. "All right, mister. It was a fair fight. But I want to talk to you. In my office. And I mean now."

CHAPTER THREE

Ben walked down the street beside the lawman, avoiding the gazes of the men lounging now along the boardwalk near the express office. Some looked more dangerous than Pecos. With the fight over, more men and some ladies were in view. Ranch hands and merchants mingled along the way, and two silent Navajo men stood back from the crowd. The town, its buildings faded and weather-beaten, had the usual spread of stores and ranching supply outfits, two cafés, the Wagon Wheel Saloon, and the two-story hotel.

They reached the jailhouse, and the lawman pushed open the door to his office. Behind a wooden door that stood open in the center of the back wall, Ben spied two empty cells. In the left corner of the front office was a cot with crumpled blankets, obviously where the lawman slept. Coffee steamed on the iron stove opposite the cot, with a table and chairs nearby. A desk on the right half of the office faced one of the two front windows. The side walls were solid planking except for rifle slots, and high above each cell in the back room was a narrow, barred window.

The lawman poured them both coffee. He handed Ben one chipped cup, then sat at his desk and motioned Ben to sit across from him. Uneasy, Ben sat down, gazing at the man's badge. It read *Deputy U.S. Marshal.*

The lawman sipped his coffee. "I'm Bob Reilly. I've been expecting you."

He recognized the name. Reilly was the marshal who'd written to him. "Ben Hawks. Who's the Pecos Kid?"

"Gunman been hanging around town. No one's sure who paid his way. I never saw his face on any handbill. He makes a lot of trouble, mostly when I'm out of town, but today, seems like he couldn't resist."

"I could have done without him."

"You did the town a favor," Reilly said. "But that's not why you came here."

Ben nodded. "Got your letter in Texas. You said you might have information about the '76 stage robbery."

"That was a bad one, all right." Reilly leaned forward. "And so much loot, Avery and his whole gang just up and disappeared afterward."

Ben stared into his steaming cup as Reilly continued. "I heard you had it out with two of Avery's men not too long ago."

"Yeah. They're dead and buried."

"Got 'em both at the same time." Reilly sounded impressed.

Ben shrugged. "Didn't give me no choice."

"They say what Avery looks like?"

"All I got out of 'em was, he was dead."

"You believe it?"

"No." Ben sipped his coffee and tried not to think back.

Reilly made a face. "The odd thing is, every one of Avery's gang was fiercely loyal to Avery. Most gangs, you get a couple-three who'll turn in the head honcho over some falling-out, or because they want to take over. Not with Avery, though. Likely on account of he made them a lot of money. No telling how many of 'em are still out there along with Avery. I'm told he had as many as two dozen riders at various times."

Ben drew a deep breath, then spoke with long-buried pain. He had come a long way from Texas with the expectation of news that would help him. "So why am I here?"

The lawman fondled his cup. "Well, first off, there's been trouble brewing between the two Kendall brothers on their ranch and the Larabee spread. A couple months back, Laird Kendall was shot dead out on his own place. A couple weeks ago, a Larabee cowhand calling himself Rossiter was shot in the back on the Larabee range. Maybe in retaliation." Reilly reached into his desk drawer and pulled out an envelope, then took something from it. He handed over a man's ornate gold watch. A gold chain dangled from it. "When Rossiter was brought in, I confiscated this," Reilly said. "It belonged to the driver from the '76 stage robbery."

Ben stared at the watch in his hand. The slick, cold feel of it brought back the horrible story the station manager had related, about how Lora and the other passengers met their end. He swallowed hard. Abruptly, he stood and paced around the office. It felt hard to breathe. He paced some more, then sat back down, still gazing at the shiny gold object in his hand. "How do you know it belonged to the driver?"

Reilly gestured at it. "Look on the back. You can see how the owner's name was scratched off, but they weren't bright enough to pop open the back cover and look inside. The watch has an identification number, along with the jeweler's address in Santa Fe and the date. Turned out it was a gift from the driver's father."

Ben swallowed hard once more, but the lump remained in his throat. A sweet and beautiful woman, ever in his heart, would never return. After three years, he could barely remember her face, but his lost love had settled like a rock in his gut, prodding him to keep riding and searching.

"Rossiter may have been right there with Avery," Reilly said.

Ben thought of the terrible story the relay station manager had told him about the stage rolling downhill. How crushed and battered must Lora's body have been? Someone had to pay for those six lives. For Lora's suffering. Avery had to be punished or shot dead, however Avery wanted it.

He reluctantly returned the watch as the lawman continued. "If Rossiter really was one of Avery's riders, he probably gambled away most of his share and had to find honest work for a while. The barkeep said as how he was lousy at cards. Then again, he could have won the watch in a card game. Even losers win sometimes."

"Where'd Rossiter come from?"

"I never found out for sure, but his face wasn't on any handbills," Reilly said. "He was riding the grub line when Larabee hired him."

"You don't think he came here to be around Avery?"

"That's wishful thinking."

Ben grimaced. "You know this Larabee fellow?"

"Yeah, Hack Larabee."

Startled, Ben sat back. "The outlaw?"

"You could say that. But I heard he was first in his class at West Point and bound for big things before the War Between the States broke out. He ended up a major in the Confederate cavalry."

"And then?"

"They say his wife died while he was fighting in Tennessee, and his son died at Franklin with another outfit. So he was already a bitter man when it was over. After that, he and his brother and some other Rebs refused to surrender, and they caused a lot of trouble. Robbing banks, mostly."

"I thought they went to prison."

"Well, they turned themselves in, thinking they was getting amnesty, and some did, but Larabee and his brother got singled out and sent up. His brother died in prison."

"And now?"

"Hack got out in '74 with a full pardon from President Grant.

I heard Grant figured their being refused amnesty was a vindictive reaction to the war and unfair to men who had served honorably for their own cause. Too late for his brother, but Hack ended up here in late '76."

Ben felt his muscles tense. "After the Tucson stage robbery? Where'd he get the money for his ranch?"

"I don't know. But he's a family man, of a sort. His brother left a daughter, lives with Hack."

"Maybe Hack Larabee's also Brian Avery."

"It ain't likely," the lawman replied. "I understand Hack was well regarded by both sides in the war. And I'm told no one really knows where Avery came from or if he fought for the North or South. Avery's always been like a ghost."

"Just the same, it's a real coincidence," Ben said. "Larabee's out in '74. Avery's name shows up in '75. And the Tucson stage was robbed in spring of '76. Then Larabee buys a ranch here in late '76, two years at most out of prison."

Reilly shook his head. "I don't see him as Avery."

Ben adjusted his hat. "Even though he had an outlaw gang himself?"

"That's true," Reilly said. "But Hack doesn't have that brutal mentality. He growls some, but his bark's worse than his bite. And the closest Avery ever came around here was way down in Mesilla in '75, about the time we first heard of him. They got one of his men in the middle of a robbery, but somebody busted the fellow out of jail and he was never seen again. This was a year before the Tucson holdup."

"That may be the first we knew Avery's name, but he still could have been operating since the war."

Reilly balanced his cup. "The few of his men that had faces on posters, they were killed at one time or another, including the two you got. But the rest of the gang, who knows who they are or what they look like?"

"If Rossiter was one of them, the rest could be around here, too. Skunks hang together, and they can't hide their stripes for long. Anyone here with a lot of money?"

"Well," Reilly said, "the Kendalls came here last year with a lot of cash to buy their spread, but word is their family is pretty rich back East. A few others in town seem well heeled, but no one stands out." He sipped coffee and settled back in his chair, a bit more subdued. "But you're right that men like Avery's gang are drawn to trouble spots, and we got a range war brewing hereabouts between Hack Larabee's Crooked Spur and the Kendalls' Lazy K. Killing Rossiter had to be retaliation for Laird Kendall being ambushed. It could escalate."

Ben shrugged. "Don't sound like the Kendalls have any connection with Avery, or else why kill Rossiter, if he was one of the gang?"

"We don't know anything for sure." Reilly shoved the watch back in his desk drawer. "Laird Kendall and his brother Miles came from Boston. Gentlemen ranchers. The only reason they got to buy their spread was, the former owner wouldn't sell it to Larabee because he'd been a reb. And then last spring, Laird met a pretty woman off the stage, and they were married in June. Big shindig. Invited the whole valley."

Ben drank his coffee and paid attention as the lawman went on.

"So there you have it. Kendalls buy their ranch from Larabee's neighbor and then they try to buy out Larabee, but Hack blows his cork. Then Laird Kendall has a big wedding in June. He gets dry-gulched a few weeks later, and Rossiter right after. I don't know why the trouble started between the Kendalls and the Crooked Spur except on account of Larabee was mad he couldn't buy that spread, and then he refused to sell his own place to the Kendalls."

"So they don't like each other," Ben said.

27

"You got that right."

"Who works for Hack Larabee?"

"No one fancy. No hired guns like the Kendalls seem to collect. But he's got a tough fellow named Sloan running things. And of course, Hack's a fair hand with a gun himself. So's his niece, by the way."

"What about the Kendalls?"

"Laird Kendall left a right pretty widow. And Laird's kid brother, Miles, he's been courting Larabee's niece. I think he figures to marry onto Larabee's spread. But to answer your question, the Lazy K has a number of gun hands can't swing a rope. And a ramrod who'd slit your throat at the drop of a hat. Fellow named Harry Frye."

Ben shook his head at the name. "You're the only law around?"

"Whenever I can get here."

"And the army?"

"Don't see much of 'em. Sometimes up from Fort Bayard. Or down from Wingate. We're too far off the beaten path. We get the stage once or twice a week if we're lucky. Every couple of weeks, the circuit judge swings by. And the only reason we got a doctor is, his pa owns the saloon. I figure things might change with the railroad, because it'll flood the territory with settlers. It's already at Raton Pass and headed for Santa Fe."

Ben emptied his cup and set it down. "Anyone else know about the watch?"

"Yeah, but I told 'em it was stolen from some drummer passing through, and I was sending it on to him."

The strong coffee had charged Ben with new energy. "How do I get to the Larabee ranch?"

"Due north into the hills," Reilly said. "Then follow along the big creek, upstream. But watch yourself. Your reputation is no secret."

"It's become a burden."

"I can imagine. I've seen some of those dime novels."

Ben nodded, embarrassed.

"So what are you going to tell Larabee?" Reilly asked.

"Just who I am, see if it makes him nervous. I'll try to hire on, see what I can find out."

"He'd grab the chance to hire Ben Hawks, that's for sure. But that also means you may be riding into a lot of trouble."

"Whatever flushes 'em out."

CHAPTER FOUR

"You know, you might think about going back to the rangers," Reilly said to Ben as they walked out of the jail into the morning sunlight.

"McNelly died a couple years ago. I don't figure things would be the same for me now."

"Wearing twin holsters like that can get right heavy on a man."

Ben nodded. "But saved my life a few times."

The crowd had dispersed, except for three boys peering out of an alley for a look at the fast gun who beat the Pecos Kid. The boardwalk creaked under Ben's boots as he turned to go around the wagon in front of the rail. He paused as a tall man approached.

The stranger wore a fancy store-bought suit with a red vest, a diamond stickpin, and a black string tie. Bare-headed, with curly brown hair, he came strolling toward them as if he owned the town. He had pale blue eyes, his handsome face set in a friendly smile. He wore a black gun belt under his coat. He looked nigh on forty, and as vain as any man could be.

"Good morning, Marshal," the stranger said. He spoke with an eastern accent, in a silky voice that matched his dapper outfit and raised Ben's hackles. "You do keep busy."

Reilly's tone was carefully neutral. "Chandler Strong, this here's Ben Hawks."

Ben did not offer his hand, nor did Chandler. Instead,

Chandler drew a long cigar from the pocket of his suit jacket. "Oh, yes, I saw the gunfight. You live up to your reputation, Mr. Hawks. And if you're heading for the Larabees' place, pay my respects to Miss Roxanna, will you?" He smiled, turned around, and headed back down the boardwalk, bowing to two women as they came out of a store. Then he crossed over and entered the saloon.

Reilly was frowning. "Quite a dandy," Ben said. "He needs a good dunking in the dirt."

The joke lightened the lawman's grim look. "He comes across as a snob," Reilly agreed. "And he's a real dude. Maybe he's just gullible, but he has some nasty friends. Pecos spent a lot of time around him."

The saloon doors swung open, and a rough-looking man came out. Well-built and strong, he wore a rawhide vest and a tied-down holster, and sported a scar on his cheek. He didn't look their way as he strolled up the street. He had a strut to his walk and wore big Mexican spurs that jingled. His way of getting attention, Ben guessed.

"That's Hatcher," Reilly said. "Another gunman, works for the Kendalls. Seems to be pretty independent of 'em, comes to town, hangs around. But I don't think he's real fast or on the prod. He thinks he's God's gift to women and spends a lot of time going to other towns looking for painted ladies. We don't have any here."

Ben couldn't have cared less. He started toward the wagon parked in front of the rail, eager to head out to Hack Larabee's place and take the man's measure. *See for myself if he might be Brian Avery.* His impatience must have shown, because Reilly forestalled him with a touch on the shoulder. "You outdrew Pecos," Reilly said, "and he was the fastest one around. I don't think anyone's going to be in a hurry to take you face on, so if I were you, I'd watch my back."

31

More than a few cowards had taken shots at Ben over the years, just missing him from ambush. He had more respect for men who faced him, even the hard cases. Yet he knew the lawman was right. Killing Pecos had likely opened the door to a lot of trouble.

"Lucky thing about Hatcher," Reilly added as they watched the big man go into the hotel up the street. "You can hear him coming with those ridiculous spurs."

"He must know it," Ben said.

"Yeah, and he's always bragging that when he runs out of painted ladies, he's going to find the right woman, fall in love, and give them to her." Reilly clearly got such a kick out of the thought, Ben almost broke a smile.

They walked around the wagon and across to where Ben's horse stood by the express office. "So what about Chandler Strong?" Ben asked.

The lawman grunted. "He seems to have a lot of money. Way he talks, he's from back East somewhere. And he's another one courting Larabee's niece."

When they reached Ben's chestnut gelding, Reilly ran his hand over the horse's long neck and into the white mane. "This is one beautiful animal. Man has a horse like this, he can't be all bad. What do you call him?"

"Texas."

Reilly grinned. "Why am I not surprised?"

Ben tightened the cinch and dropped the stirrup.

"You're not giving him a rest?" Reilly said.

"I've grain in my possible sack. I just want to get out of town."

Reilly nodded. "I understand."

Further up the street, three empty freight wagons with double teams were pulling out to head east. Two riders rode around the wagons to lead, while a third rider turned and headed toward Reilly and Ben.

"Here's another one after Hack's niece," Reilly said. "He got here a few months ago, doing a big business hauling freight. Chad Gorman. From somewhere back East, like the others, I reckon."

Gorman was big and brawny, and wore range clothes but looked like another dude with his fancy kerchief, striped vest, and brand-new hat. He had clear brown eyes and dark hair, neatly cropped. Ben guessed his age at close to forty.

"Marshal," Gorman said with a wide smile, "I just had to meet your friend."

"Ben Hawks," Reilly said. "Ben, this here's Chad Gorman."

"I missed the fight," Gorman said, catching Ben's eye, "but I wanted to thank you."

Ben pushed his hat back and nodded, even though killing a man had never been a source of pride. Gorman looked like a decent man, just the same.

The freight hauler looked at Reilly again. "Marshal, if you should see Miss Roxanna, tell her I'll be back."

"Are you headed for Santa Fe?" Reilly asked.

"The wagons are. I'm just going to Nickel's Farm." Gorman tipped his hat and turned his horse, riding to catch up with the wagons.

"Nickel's son, he's another one," Reilly said. "Been up north a few years and just got back to help with the farm and dairy. Seems steady enough. Educated fellow. He's been calling on Miss Larabee as well."

"Is everyone?" Ben asked.

"Yeah, well, ain't many single ladies way out here, and she's not only real pretty, she owns half a ranch. They all want to get their foot in the door. Chandler Strong, Chad Gorman, young Nickel. And a couple others what have less chance. I'd put my money on Gorman."

Ben mounted, then leaned down to shake the lawman's hand.

Reilly clasped it firmly. "You play it straight, Ben, and you got a friend in me."

"Thanks." It felt good to know that. Ben related well to most lawmen, as his father had been one, and with the rangers, Ben had thought he'd found a life fitted for him. But Reilly had a little more to him than most. Someone he could rely on if he needed to.

He let go of the marshal's hand and turned his gelding north, out of town.

Hatcher walked out of the hotel and headed for the livery across the street. He looked back at the jail but saw no sign of the lawman. Marshal Reilly must've gone back into his office.

No one had ordered Hatcher on this ride. It just happened to be part of his job. He also enjoyed causing trouble, like firing at the dirt to make a man dance. People said he had a weird sense of humor that didn't play well with others. He guessed that was true, and it didn't bother him any.

In the livery barn, Hatcher claimed his bay horse. He sat down on a box, took off his spurs, and shoved them inside his tack, which he kept in the stall. As he led his horse out of the enclosure, the livery owner came walking over. Stooped and lame, Pete had no hair but a lot of curiosity. More than was good for him, Hatcher thought.

"Mr. Hatcher, you want to sell them spurs?" Pete asked.

Hatcher shook his head as he saddled his bay.

"I missed the gunfight," Pete said. "Did you see it?"

Hatcher nodded as he tightened the cinch and dropped the stirrup.

Pete's helper, a teenage boy with freckles and too much curly blonde hair, came forward to join the conversation. "I saw it," the boy said. "No one can take Ben Hawks."

Hatcher mounted and gave them an icy look. They backed

off as he rode out, which lifted his mood. He liked to scare everyone in sight.

With the sun already high in the afternoon sky, Ben rode north toward the distant, wooded hills, beyond which rose crimson cliffs and the dark blue mountains to the north and west. Twice this day, the past had been dredged up, tearing him apart. He needed to be alone in the lush hills and fresh, clean air.

His horse easily crossed the waving grassland and followed the wagon road along the wide, sandy creek. It led into grassy hills where he saw clumps of gray-green junipers and tall, dark pinyon pine, cones already open. Golden aspens with shimmering leaves clustered among them. Ben rested his mount with grain and some water from the stream. He brushed Tex down, rubbed the horse's back, and checked its shoes. After that, he permitted himself a few bites of jerky and a rest. Killing any man, even one like Pecos, took a lot out of him, and he wondered if he would ever return to a decent life. He thought of Luke, and what his friend had said. Yet Ben felt he could never revert to the young, spirited ranger who had once been a happy man.

He mounted up again and continued his ride. The warm sun and glorious scenery gave him momentary peace. After a while he saw hoof marks of cattle and horses along the stream. A black, lazy buzzard with its bare red head and V-shaped wings cruised in the western sky and disappeared beyond the ridge. "Same one as this morning, I'll bet," Ben said.

Tex's ears twitched as if the horse understood.

Something rustled in the wiry brush along the sparkling creek. Tex shied as a large wild turkey, nearly four feet long, flew out in front of him. Glossy brown with red wattles, it sailed across the creek. Its long tail had a black band near the tip. It landed beyond another stand of yellow-flowering brush and disappeared.

As Ben fought to control his mount, a shot rang out. Ben felt it whistle past his face. He dived from the saddle and into the trees, Tex following right behind.

Another shot hit the tree next to him. He pulled his Winchester repeater from its scabbard and squinted toward a nearby rise of rocks where sunlight glinted off a rifle barrel. As he watched, it drew out of sight.

Ben positioned himself against a tree trunk and waited. Another shot rang out, chipping bark from above his head. He squinted at the rocks, saw a hat brim near where the rifle had shown. He fired. The hat dropped out of sight, followed by more shooting. This time, the shot hit a different tree.

Ben fired back rapidly, hitting the rocks. A dark figure scurried away through the boulders and out of sight. Ben waited until he caught a glimpse of a man riding off. A bay horse, a large-built rider. Too far away and too much cover to see who it was.

Tex stood a few feet distant amid the trees, snorting and upset but unhurt. As Ben calmed his gelding, he heard hoofbeats. He looked northward and saw four riders heading his way. The man in the rocks must have seen them coming.

Ben shoved his rifle back in the scabbard and mounted, then rode out of the trees toward the oncoming riders. As they drew closer, he saw they were cowhands. When they spotted him, they turned and rode back the way they'd come, out of sight.

In the silence, Ben looked back toward the rocks where his attacker had hidden. He urged his horse toward them and dismounted for a look around, but found no trace of the unknown gunman. Disappointed, he swung back into the saddle and continued north, but kept to the trees as long as he could.

By midafternoon, the busy creek led him through a wide pass

and into the vast valley where the Crooked Spur ranch lay. Crossbreed cattle mixed with restless longhorns across a sea of waving grass. There were riders on the far ridge, ranch buildings on the flats to the north, and a sparkling brook to Ben's left with clumps of cottonwoods nearby, their narrow leaves already turned yellow.

The sound of an approaching horse drew his attention. He turned his head and saw a rider coming out of the golden aspens to his right. On a big bay and carrying a Winchester rifle across his saddle, the man wore a scowl that threatened trouble.

"Hold it, mister," he growled.

CHAPTER FIVE

The man facing Ben on the Larabee range looked rough and menacing. A swarthy fellow around fifty or so, he had dark eyes, a wide but tight-lipped mouth under a graying black mustache, and a crooked scar on his chin. Ben guessed the four riders who witnessed the firefight by the creek had reported to him, certainly to someone. Clearly, this man didn't want strangers on the ranch.

"What business you got here?" the man snarled as he reined up near Ben.

"I came to see Mr. Larabee."

"Another fast gun, eh? You're all alike. And the Pecos Kid just wipes you out, one at a time. You take my advice, you'll head on back where you come from. I'm getting tired of burying the likes of you."

Ben studied him a long moment. "I came to see Mr. Larabee, and I'm not leaving until I do."

The man took Ben's measure in turn, then gave a grudging nod. "I'm Sloan, foreman of this here outfit. You'd better follow me. Maybe I can keep you alive until we get to the house."

"You're a real friendly sort."

Ben hadn't cracked a smile in the last several years, but he hadn't lost his sense of humor, even if Sloan didn't appreciate it. In fact, Ben liked the foreman on sight, having ridden with men like him in Texas. Best not to let Sloan know this, though. Not until he had some idea of how the land lay.

Sloan grimaced. "Don't make fun with me, mister." Grimly, he turned his horse and headed north across the valley, Ben trailing. They rode through some of the cattle, a few longhorns and the rest mixed breeds.

Sloan waved to riders on the faraway ridge and turned his bay out of the herd. He rode like a man born to the saddle, the kind of cowhand who rode for the brand and lived for his job. In the late afternoon warm with bright sun, a cold breeze began to rise. Abruptly, Sloan reined in, and Ben moved up beside him.

Riding a man's saddle on a blue roan mare, a young woman in gray jacket and flowing black skirts approached at a walk from the far woods. She wore a man's wide-brimmed hat and a red checkered bandanna at her throat. She was young, Ben noticed as she drew closer, likely in her late twenties. And gorgeous, with lustrous auburn hair blowing in the wind and flashing dark brown eyes in her pretty face. She had a rifle in a scabbard and looked ready to use it.

Ben had never seen the like of her. Any man would fall all over himself at the sight of her. Ben had a little more restraint from his years of riding the vengeance trail, but he felt something stir within him as she rode closer.

"Don't get no ideas," Sloan snapped. "Them women's saddles got no place for a rifle, and she rides herd like the rest of us. And she's a real lady. Don't you forget it."

The young woman's full skirts whipped about her boots. She rode straight in the saddle as the wind blew her shining hair about her face.

Ben and Sloan both touched their hat brims as she reined up in front of them. "Miss Larabee, this here fellow's come to see your uncle," Sloan said. "Another one of them guns what can't work a cow."

She looked Ben over, then drew herself up. "Thank you, Mr.

Sloan. I'll handle this."

Sloan grunted, reined his bay about, and headed back toward the herd.

Ben shifted his weight in the saddle. This must be Roxanna Larabee. He could read her glaring assessment of him and found himself enjoying her bravado.

"Who are you?" she demanded.

It took him a moment to answer. "Ben Hawks."

Taken aback, she hesitated, then snapped at him. "Oh, yes, the man in the songs. Well, Uncle Hack's not hiring any more of your kind, so you'd best ride on out."

"Excuse me, ma'am, but my business is with your uncle."

One hand drifted near her rifle. "I'm telling you to turn and ride out of here before I put a hole in you."

Ben found himself wanting to smile. He pushed his hat back from his damp brow. "I bet you could do that without shedding a tear."

"That's exactly right."

He hid his amusement at her challenge. "I'm not about to leave until I see your uncle, so start shooting," he said.

She continued to glare at him. "All right, but I'm warning you. We don't want any killers on our payroll."

Ben thought of her uncle and father, ex-Confederate officers, wanted men for many years, alleged murderers and thieves. Losing his son in the war and his wife while they were away, then being denied amnesty and with his brother dying in prison, all of it would likely have made Hack Larabee a bitter man. He couldn't forget Hack had been out of prison in '74, and Brian Avery had made his name as an outlaw a year later. Also, Hack bought this very ranch a year after the Tucson stage robbery that cost Lora her life.

If Hack and Brian Avery were the same man, Ben would soon have the smell of it.

Roxanna tugged at her hat, turned her roan, and headed north. Ben rode alongside. He admired her spunk, and even more the flow of her hair. Brown with red highlights, it reached nearly to her waist. Next to her in the warm sun, surrounded by crimson and yellow ridges, dark pinyon pine and creeks splashing along the way, Ben couldn't help feeling the Crooked Spur had to be a good place for any man.

They soon caught sight of the ranch buildings up ahead. The barn, sheds, bunkhouse, and corrals with horses stood to the west, while the Texas-style main house stood on a knoll eastward, backed by shimmering golden aspens. A one-story building of timber and adobe, it was built as two long rambling structures with one roof, with an open dog trot in between. Around the buildings, rolling hills spread in all directions. Beyond the red-streaked ridges, the dark mountains, crested with snow, rose against the northern sky.

As they reined up at the corrals, Roxanna glanced at Ben's chestnut gelding with what he thought was appreciation, but she refused to offer a compliment. He could see she had no intention of giving him any quarter. After they swung down and left their horses at a corral fence, he discovered she hardly came up to his chin, but she walked tall as they crossed over toward the house and followed the path up to the dog trot. She kept ahead of him, and he allowed it because she tickled him.

She didn't look back until she entered the open space between the buildings, the roof shading them from the fading sunlight. There, she paused at the door of the larger south half of the building, her hand on the latch, looking him over again with disdain. "I hope he sends you right off."

Ben swallowed his enjoyment. A man could do a lot worse than be around this lovely woman full of spit and vinegar. He'd never get any rest, nor would he ask for it. If a man had her in his arms, he would be in Heaven and never want to come down.

Where had those thoughts come from?

She pushed the door open. He followed her into a big room with a huge stone fireplace where a log burned brightly, sap popping and crackling. The room felt cold despite the fire. It smelled of coffee, leather, and burning wood. Ben saw several pieces of leather furniture, and rifles, paintings, and hides on the walls. Hats and coats hung on a rack near the entrance. Saddles were to the left on wooden stands. Bridles and ropes hung on the horns. Beyond the main room, a hallway led to the rest of the house.

In a big leather chair in front of the fire sat a man in his mid-fifties, stocky and wearing a leather vest over his wrinkled dark blue shirt. He was hatless, with gray thinning hair and a graying brown handlebar mustache. When he turned to look at them, Ben saw rough features and a jutting chin.

Roxanna hung her hat on the rack and stalked over to him. "Uncle Hack, this gunman wants to see you."

She glared at Ben as she gestured to a chair near her uncle. Sparring with her could be a real pleasure, Ben thought. Except he had another reason for being here. He looked away from her, reminded of his search for justice.

Larabee did not stand. Ben reached down to shake his hand. "Ben Hawks."

Larabee's grin showed surprise and curiosity. "Hawks? Well, I'll be switched. Roxanna, get us some coffee, will you?"

As Ben sat near the hearth, she made a face and turned away, going into the far hallway and leaving Ben to twirl his hat in his hand. The rancher studied him. "I've heard plenty about you, Hawks. Some of those coyotes you outdrew were mighty fast guns, and I hear you ride across the sky at night."

"I heard plenty of stories about you."

Hack shrugged his big shoulders. "Yeah, well, that was a long time ago. As a man gets older, he takes a little more time to think about what he's doing and why. And the consequences."

Ben knew what he meant, as he considered where he might end up.

Roxanna returned with three steaming cups of coffee on a tray. She handed one to Ben and another to her uncle, then sat on the other side of Hack with her own cup. Conscious of her watching him, Ben sipped the hot coffee and enjoyed its flavor. The hearth felt like home, which unsettled him. He'd just met these people, couldn't say in a few minutes' acquaintance whether or not Hack was the outlaw he'd long sought. His time in the Texas Rangers had taught him a thing or two about sizing people up, though, and despite Hack Larabee's history Ben saw something in him he hadn't expected, a man who had more decency than most. Maybe what he saw came from West Point training or the Confederate cavalry, and not from the outlaw trail.

Then again, maybe he was wrong. Too soon to let his guard down.

Hack leaned forward. "So why are you here?"

"I was looking to hire on," Ben said.

"So you heard about our troubles with the Kendalls' Lazy K."

"From Marshal Reilly."

Roxanna huffed. "Uncle Hack, having a name like Ben Hawks on the payroll will just escalate everything."

"Now just a minute," Hack said. "Reilly sent him."

"Ben Hawks is a killer," she said.

Her antagonism didn't tickle him so much now. He was getting a mite tired of it. Ben refused to look at her as he sipped his coffee.

"Take a good look," Hack said to her. "Does he look like a bad man?"

She stared into her cup. "Yes."

"Stop being such a girl," Hack said.

She looked up at her uncle with flashing eyes but held her temper.

Hack balanced his cup as he crossed one leg over his knee. "We got trouble, Ben. One man dead on each side, but no one can prove who done it, and I sure didn't order it done. And there's this gunman in town, Pecos, scaring half my men whenever the marshal's gone. Some even quit after he took shots at 'em in the Wagon Wheel Saloon. We figure he's on the Lazy K's payroll, but we can't prove nothing."

Roxanna sat up straight. "Uncle Hack, Pecos has run off every gun you hired. And maybe this time, he won't bother to miss."

Hack ignored her. "If you work for us, it'd be good for the men's morale, so yeah, I'd like to hire you. Your name on the payroll alone might scare the Kendalls off. And you could watch our backs, me and Roxanna. Not looking for you to pick any fights, but it wouldn't hurt if you could make Pecos back down."

"I don't need a bodyguard," Roxanna snapped.

"Roxanna, don't you have some knitting to do?"

She half rose out of her chair. "Uncle Henry, you know I work as hard as any man on this ranch. I don't have time for knitting."

He scowled. "Don't call me Henry."

She settled back down. "You said I was a partner, so I have something to say about hiring any gunfighter."

"Well, maybe he's just what we need around here. And you were a Texas Ranger, right, Ben?"

Ben nodded, then downed his coffee and stared into the flames. He felt suddenly weary and a lot older than his thirty years.

"Well," Hack said, "that's good enough for me."

She fumed. "Pecos will go crazy when he hears about Ben Hawks."

"Pecos won't come on our ranch," Hack said.

Chin up, she shot back, "We need to make peace, not war."

"Honey, I know Miles Kendall's been courting you, but that won't stop the killing. In fact, he's likely blaming us for his brother's death. How do we know what he's planning? I figure we need Ben here to watch my back and keep an eye on you."

"I can take care of myself," she snapped.

Hack turned to Ben. "Now, Ben, I know you likely been paid a lot more, but we just want you to hang around, so a hundred a month for starters?"

Ben nodded and balanced his empty cup. Should he tell them about Pecos? He hated the thought of it, hated that he'd had to kill the man. Before he could say a word, Hack addressed his niece. "Roxanna, fix him up on the other side of the house in the storeroom. There's a cot in there."

"What about the bunkhouse?" she asked, startled.

"He ain't here to herd cows. I want him to keep us alive. And he can't do it from there. Besides, I get lonesome for something besides female company."

"You're making a mistake, Uncle Henry."

Hack Larabee's dark eyes narrowed. "I'm the boss around here."

She stood up in anger. "So let him make his own bed."

"All right, but at least you can bring us some more coffee."

"He works for you. Let him get it."

Hack glanced Ben's way. "Ben, if you've a mind, get us some more coffee. I don't figure my partner's going to accommodate us."

Ben fought back a smile and stood up, taking both cups. He paused to enjoy her haughty glare, then went down the far hallway to the next room where he found a large iron stove, a big coffee pot steaming on the side, and a rough-hewn dining room table. He filled the cups, then turned, about to reenter the hallway, when he heard sudden pounding on the front door. He paused, out of sight.

Light footsteps sounded as Roxanna went to open the door. Ben moved to the kitchen doorway and watched as a freckle-faced cowhand, barely twenty years old if that, came charging inside. Bright with excitement, the cowhand fought for breath. He held his hat in his hand as he ran his fingers through his blonde hair. "Miss Roxanna, you wouldn't believe what happened!" He accompanied her into the main room. Curiosity roused, Ben followed them, and paused by the entrance just out of view.

Roxanna retreated to the hearth. Hack remained in his big chair. "What is it got you so stirred up, Buckley?" he said.

The young hand was still breathing hard, as if he'd run a long way. "Mr. Larabee, I just come back from town. I had to sit around so long for the supplies. And I could hardly wait to get here."

"Calm down, Buckley. Start at the beginning, why don't you."

Buckley nodded. "I was at the general store this morning, and the Pecos Kid was causing a lot of trouble and scaring everybody like he always does." He caught his breath again and continued. "Then Pecos gets in the street all of a sudden when a stranger comes riding in, and Pecos calls out the stranger's name real loud—'Hawks!' You know . . . Ben Hawks, that gunfighter from Texas, and ole Pecos, he was figuring on running Hawks out of town."

Hack stared at him. Roxanna sat down, twisting a lock of her long hair in her fingers. Buckley's face was flushed red with the thrill of his story.

"Hawks just turned his back, but Pecos kept after 'im and went on insulting 'im. Ole Hawks got mighty uptight but he still didn't turn around, just kept on ignoring him, while everybody in town, they took cover."

He paused, and Hack said, "Well, spit it out."

"It got worse when ole Pecos said Hawks' mother was part Comanche." Buckley swallowed, then twirled his hat. "Hawks, he turns around and goes out in the street real slow, and he sure looks mean. They face each other out there, and everybody's hiding real scared, 'cause they know how fast ole Pecos is." He caught his breath again. "Pecos, he throws up this here silver dollar to start the fight, but before it hits the ground, he goes for his gun."

Hack grimaced. "Buckley, just get it said."

"Well, ole Hawks, he draws and shoots so fast, nobody even sees his hand move, and Pecos drops like a sack of wheat. I tell you, it was really something. Never thought nobody could outdraw ole Pecos."

Hack stared at him. "Pecos is dead?"

"Not right then, on account of he was hit in the shoulder, and they were gonna take him to the doctor, but when Hawks turned his back, Pecos, he grabbed his gun in both hands and turned around and was gonna kill Hawks right then." Buckley paused and took another deep breath.

"Hawks ain't dead," Hack snapped.

"No," Buckley said, "but Pecos is. Hawks, he spun around and drew real fast and shot Pecos dead center." He shook his head in wonderment. "Ole Hawks must have eyes in the back of his head."

Roxanna leaned back, shock and dismay on her face. Hack tugged at his mustache, his mouth twisting into a sudden grin. "Glory be. All right, Buckley, thanks."

Buckley started backing toward the entrance. "Yeah, but maybe now Kendall's gonna try to hire Ben Hawks."

"We'll see about that," Hack said with a chuckle. The young

cowhand left, and Hack just grinned while Roxanna steamed.

Ben, sober-faced, slowly entered the room with the two cups of coffee. He still regretted killing Pecos, but kind of enjoyed that it so irked Roxanna.

Roxanna stood up, glaring at him. "Why didn't you tell us you shot Pecos? Were you trying to get money for something you'd already done?"

Hack chuckled again. "Roxanna, calm down. It seems our Mr. Hawks ain't one to brag, that's all."

Ben came over and handed Hack a cup, then sat down with his own. He still didn't crack a smile, but let it show in his eyes how much he enjoyed her complaint.

Hack settled back. "Well, now. With Pecos out of the way, we'll have a rest, but if the Kendalls was paying 'im, they'll call in someone else, you can bet on it."

Still angry, Roxanna muttered, "I have work to do." She spun on her heel and grabbed her hat and coat, then went to the front door, jerked it open, and charged outside, slamming it behind her.

Hack chuckled. "You sure got her dander up."

"She don't like me, that's for sure."

"She don't have to, Ben."

"Marshal said Miles Kendall's after her. And that dandy I met in town, Chandler Strong."

Hack made a face. "They ain't the only ones, but they're the most persistent. Kendalls come from Boston, some high-tone family, and probably bought their way out of service. Chandler's got an eastern accent. All Yankees."

"So you're still fighting the war."

The rancher shrugged. "It's been what, fourteen years? Some things a man can't throw away, Ben, and if it wasn't for my niece, no telling where I'd be." An expression crossed his face right then as if he'd said too much and regretted it. "But right now, you've had a hard ride. Why don't you get some rest? Go on through to the other side of the house. Take the last room you come to. It has a back door. Oughta be some blankets in there. And a lamp."

"Thanks."

"We'll be having supper right after sundown."

"Your niece doing the cooking?"

"Yeah, are you worried?"

"Sure am."

Larabee chuckled. "I'm going to enjoy having you around."

Ben wished he could say the same. He liked this man on instinct, but wasn't sure of him yet. "I'll get my gear and take care of my horse."

Hack sobered as Ben stood up. "A lot of men got their eye on Roxanna. You keep a sharp lookout, Ben. Maybe I'm a doting uncle, but I ain't seen one yet worthy of shining her boots."

"Whatever you say, Mr. Larabee."

"Call me Hack. And while you're at it, maybe you can tell me why you're really here. A hundred a month ain't much for a fast gun like you. You quit the rangers, but you've been riding a really hard trail from what I heard."

Hat in hand, Ben forced himself to stay calm. Hack Larabee was quicker than he'd thought. Ben hesitated, shrugged, could not find the words.

Hack gave him a look, long enough to make Ben's mouth go dry. Then he nodded. "All right, Ben. As long as you remember you're riding for the brand."

"I'll remember."

CHAPTER SIX

At sunset on the Lazy K, Miles Kendall and his ramrod were out at the ranch corrals.

A big man in his late forties with a handsome but swarthy face and a cleft in his clean-shaven chin, Miles wore a leather coat with a wool collar, his hat pushed back. He had never been a cattleman, but he liked the ranch life as long as others did the work.

Frye, the ramrod, had heavy dark eyebrows and sported a black mustache over his wide, thin lips. A stocky man in his forties, he had a glint in his dark eyes. He was more educated than most men out here, but only fools thought him soft because of it. He wore his six-gun tied down and made no one doubt he could use it.

Even when Frye smiled, Miles could never be sure the expression was genuine. More like a dog that needed worming. Or a man with secrets, Miles often thought.

As the twilight slowly gathered, Miles glanced over at the two-story ranch house with its wide, covered front porch. Lamps glowed in the windows. He knew his brother's widow waited inside with her maid. She must miss Laird as much as he did, probably more. Laird Kendall had been the elder brother and their father's favorite, which Miles had resented even as he looked up to Laird. Now, as the only remaining son, he received letters and encouragement from their father and mother, especially with regard to his courting Roxanna Larabee. More than anything right now, he wanted to marry her.

In the fading light, he and Frye leaned on the corral fence watching the new mares they had just bought.

"That sorrel is carrying," Frye said.

"Then we were cheated. What about that stud you were getting from Santa Fe?"

Frye shrugged. "Turned us down, but there's another I know of."

Just then, one of the men came riding from the direction of town. Katz, his name was. A chunky man with a short beard and crooked nose, he reined up and leaned on the pommel in the moonlight.

Miles didn't particularly like Katz. The man only took direction from Frye, which might be understandable given Frye's position at the Lazy K. But he always felt Katz had looked down on him and his late brother, seeing them as dudes not worthy of a real cowman's consideration. Worse, Katz always seemed to be laughing behind everyone's backs.

At the moment, he looked and sounded out of breath as he pushed his hat back.

"Where are the other men?" Frye said.

"Coming, but I had to get here and tell you about Pecos."

"What about him?"

Both Miles and Frye stood waiting in the twilight. Katz took his time before answering, a big grin on his face as if savoring the story he had to tell. The pale moonlight and twinkling stars added to the mood as Katz finally spoke. "Pecos is dead. Shot down in a gunfight."

"Not possible," Frye said. "Or wasn't it fair and square?"

"Well, Pecos drew first."

Miles shook his head. "This sure isn't Boston."

Frye looked irritated. No one had liked Pecos, but he'd made himself useful running roughshod over Larabee riders whenever

51

the marshal rode out of town. No one else fit the job. "Who the devil could take Pecos?"

"Ben Hawks," Katz said, sobering.

Stunned, Frye could only stare at him. "Nobody's that fast. Not even Ben Hawks, except in dime novels."

"Who's Ben Hawks?" Miles asked.

"He's the hunter," Katz told him. "From Texas. The one who rides the night sky. Which is probably how he got here."

"Hunter? What do you mean? Who does he hunt?" Miles persisted.

"Who knows, but every one of us got to worry."

The night's chill drew on as Katz went over the gunfight in great detail, including how Pecos cheated, along with how he tried to shoot Hawks in the back and ended up dead himself. "Not long after that, Hawks went out to the Crooked Spur. I'm betting old Hack Larabee's hired him on."

"Yes," Frye said, looking not at all surprised. "Larabee would hire a Texan."

"Maybe you can still get him," Katz suggested. Frye scowled and waved him away. Katz turned his horse toward the tack room beyond the barn.

Alone with Miles again in the moonlight, Frye set about rolling a smoke. "I don't believe it," he said. "Pecos was the fastest gun around, next to me."

Miles let out a sigh. "I want an end to this."

Frye smiled. "I could take Ben Hawks."

"That's not what I meant. I don't want any more fighting. And we need you here to run the ranch. Laird and I were never cattlemen."

"You'd let your brother's killer ride free?"

"We don't know who it was."

"Except whoever shot Laird had to be paid by Hack Larabee," Frye said, lighting his smoke. "And now Larabee's gone and hired Ben Hawks."

Miles, getting exasperated, adjusted his hat. "Don't do anything about Hawks. You work for the Lazy K, and they'd put the blame on me for any more trouble, so stay out of it."

"You're the boss, but we could send for Dejado."

Miles frowned, wishing Frye would leave it. "Who is he?"

"Hired gun I know. He's a bit loco, but he can take Ben Hawks easy."

"No, it's gone far enough. No more killing."

"Hawks may not agree with you."

"Forget about him. My brother wanted to buy the Crooked Spur and got turned down. I plan to marry it."

"You have a lot of competition, I hear," Frye said.

"I know what I'm doing. No more violence."

Frye nodded toward the house. "What about Mrs. Kendall?"

"She's still grieving, but I know she wants peace in the valley."

"So you're not doing anything about Ben Hawks?"

Further annoyed, Miles shook his head. "Maybe Larabee hired him, we don't know. But I know I can make a deal."

"A deal with Hack Larabee? Not so likely."

"Roxanna can handle him, and she wants no more trouble."

Frye puffed on his smoke, then leaned on the fence. "You're the boss."

Three words, inoffensive enough, but Miles heard the contempt in them. Angered and confused, he said, "Something I have to know. How is it an obviously well-educated man like yourself turned into such a hardened character?"

Frye blew smoke into the air. "Survival."

That same night, Laird Kendall's widow, Vera, thirty-four but looking years younger, stood in the parlor of the ranch house. Lamps burned bright in the well-appointed room, their light glinting off the richly polished furniture. Paintings of the West and displays of firearms adorned the walls, and a fire crackled in the huge stone fireplace.

Tired of wearing black, Vera had chosen a dark blue silk dress that set off her light blonde hair. A matching ribbon tied the pale tresses back from her face. How often Laird had admired her, complimenting her light brown eyes, delicate lips, and dimpled chin.

Behind her, the housekeeper, her black hair tied back in a red scarf, quietly went about her work. Vera paid the woman little heed until something struck the floor behind her. She turned swiftly and saw that Conchita had knocked a blue vase off of a side table with her broom handle. Luckily—for the vase and the housekeeper both—it had hit a throw rug and bounced.

Careless woman. "Pick it up, Conchita."

The housekeeper did as she was told, then turned the vase slowly in the lamplight. She was chubby, somewhere in her forties, and wore an apron over her print dress. "It is not broken, *señora.*"

Annoyed at not having a good excuse to berate her, Vera waved a hand. "All right, fine. Now get back to making supper. Miles will be hungry. And make sure you don't burn the biscuits this time. You people never learn how to do anything right."

Conchita turned her face away as she obeyed, setting the vase next to others and a heap of flowers on the side table. As the housekeeper headed back to the front room, Vera fussed with the vases and bright, mixed flowers. She culled out several yellow ones, arranged them in a white vase half full of water, and carried it over to the mantle. A minute later, her brother-in-law came wandering into the parlor. She managed a smile for him. "I'll be with you in a moment, Miles."

Hat in hand, he stretched out on a chair. "There was a big gunfight in town this morning."

"You men and your fighting. Shame on you."

"Pecos Kid bit off more than he could chew. He was shot dead."

Her back to him, she positioned the vase on the mantle, frowned, and fussed with it some more. "I thought you said no one could take Pecos."

"Well, he lost this one," Miles said. "Got outdrawn by that gunfighter from Texas. Ben Hawks."

Vera lost her grip on the vase. It fell off the mantle and shattered, hard and loud, on the stones in front of the fireplace. Flowers and water spilled at her feet. She stepped back in alarm.

Miles leaned forward. "Vera, are you all right?"

She took a moment to answer. "Yes, it was slippery, that's all."

He settled back again. "Well, it seems Hawks is going to work for Larabee."

She drew a deep breath without turning. "What are you going to do about it?"

"Nothing," he said. "I want to make peace with Larabee."

"And marry his niece?"

"Why not?"

Vera kicked white china shards into the ashes on the hearth. "She has a temper, I've heard."

He smiled. "When I met Roxanna at your wedding to my brother, I was hooked. I'll make her so happy, she won't remember she ever had a temper."

She took a deep breath. "Maybe Mr. Larabee won't agree to the marriage. Then what?"

He laughed. "Then I guess he'll send Ben Hawks after me."

She faced him then. "What?"

He sobered at her anguished voice. "I'm sorry, Vera, I didn't mean to upset you."

She moved toward the side table, where she took up more

flowers and arranged them in the blue vase Conchita had knocked over. "What about Chandler Strong? He wants to marry her, and the ranch, doesn't he?"

Miles fiddled with his hat. "Chandler Strong is a fop, a dandy and full of himself. She'd never take him seriously. Besides, you know how much Laird wanted to join the two ranches."

"Why didn't Laird marry her, then?"

Miles grinned and leaned forward in his chair. "My brother was so wild about you, he couldn't see straight. When you got off that stage in the rain and he went to help you, that was it. He was a goner. He could never see anyone else."

She kept her back to him as she toyed with the flowers. "It was the same for me. That's why I cancelled my trip to California."

Miles got to his feet. "He was so in love with you, he put your name on the deed to the Lazy K with ours, to make sure you'd be protected in case something happened to him, or both of us. That's a lot of love."

She stiffened without turning. "But you agreed."

"Sure, because Laird and I planned the same thing if I married. The laws are tough on women trying to inherit from their husbands."

"You'd put that Larabee woman's name on our ranch?"

"No need, because I'll have a share of hers."

"Hack Larabee would shoot you first."

"You underestimate my charms."

She stayed silent, all her attention on the second vase of flowers, until she heard Miles get up. "I'm sorry," he said. She could picture him fiddling with his hat. "I've upset you."

"I'm just thinking of Laird."

"I'm sorry," Miles repeated.

"It's all right, but please, I'd like to be alone."

"Sure. I'll see you at supper."

She waited until the front door closed behind him, then turned with a scowl, took up another vase, and threw it into the hearth. The loud crash drew attention. Conchita came hurriedly into the room, book in hand, and stopped.

Vera waved at the broken glass. "Clean that up." She spotted the book and sneered at it. "You people think reading will make you any smarter?"

Not waiting for an answer, Vera left the parlor and headed for the stairs.

Outside, over at the corrals, Frye watched as Hatcher rode up in the moonlight. Miles was dozing on the porch swing, out of earshot should he happen to wake up. *Just as well,* Frye thought.

Hatcher dismounted by the fence and began to unsaddle his horse. Frye thought of him and Katz as the same, both secretly laughing at everyone else. It could be right irritating.

"Where have you been?" Frye snapped at him.

"Trailing Ben Hawks out of town."

"Where was he headed?"

"The Crooked Spur."

"And?"

"Took a couple shots at him from the ridge, but some Larabee hands showed up."

Frye grimaced. "We have to get rid of him."

"If Larabee hires him, he'll be out there."

"I can't believe he outdrew Pecos."

Hatcher nodded and slung his saddle on the fence. "Pecos even cheated."

"So Katz told us."

"Hawks was just a little faster, that's all."

"And you let him get away with it?"

"Yeah. Nothing I could do. Reilly was watching."

Frye turned and looked toward the house, where lights

gleamed behind the curtains. Big Mexican spurs jingling, Hatcher led his horse into the corral and let it drink at the trough. Frye headed for his shack near the bunkhouse. He had more on his mind than Ben Hawks.

Katz came out of the barn and over to Hatcher. "You ever use those big spurs on a horse," Katz said with a grin, "you'll fly so high you'll never come down."

"Yeah, well, they impress the ladies. Makes me look tough."

Katz pushed his hat back and grunted. "Did you really take shots at Ben Hawks by the creek and miss? You can shoot better than that."

Hatcher grinned. "I just wanted to scare him. See if he could dance. But those Larabee riders showed up, so I took off."

"Brian says he wants to get rid of Hawks."

Hatcher shrugged. "Why should we take chances? I'd like to live to a ripe old age. Find me a woman, settle down."

Katz snickered. "Don't tell that to Frye."

"He feels the same but he's on the spot," Hatcher said. "He has to do what Brian tells him, but it's not easy to get around Miles Kendall."

"Miles is too busy romancing that Larabee girl."

"Him and everybody else."

"I could warm up to her," Katz said. "She'd take to me."

He and Hatcher both grinned at the joke, knowing they were whistling in the wind.

CHAPTER SEVEN

At the Larabee ranch, Ben lounged on the cot in the storeroom in the northern half of the main house. Coyote hides were hung on the walls along with several buck horns, and a bearskin rug lay on the floor. A standing rifle rack held a Sharps buffalo gun and a shotgun. Everything looked neat and clean, including the boxes and barrels of food and supplies.

With a knock on the door, Roxanna called him to supper. She sounded unfriendly, yet her voice stirred something inside of him. He had never met anyone like her. Just being around her, even when she snapped at him, gave him more pleasure than he'd had in years.

He brushed off his shirt and vest, wrapped his gun belt around his hips, clapped his hat on his head, and walked out into the dog trot. Roxanna was waiting there; she gave him a chilly glance before turning her back and leading the way to the south half of the house.

Moonlight cast a glow beyond the walk. He moved slowly behind her, thinking how strange it was to be here.

Three years ago, he was in love with Lora, so sweet and lovely she'd turned a rough young Texas Ranger into mush. He'd even helped her get the job at the express office in Austin, just to keep her around until he could work up the courage to pop the question.

When word came of the holdup, and the express company sent him the last letter he'd written her and the gold locket with their portraits inside, Ben had turned into a crazy man. Unable to bear it, he'd sent the locket to his mother and hit the vengeance trail. But Hack Larabee was right, he realized. Even though he sought justice, not vengeance, he'd grown weary of his own anger. It had drained him far too long.

And now here he was, mesmerized by a young woman he hardly knew, wanting to see her smile. Trying to annoy her so he could see the fire in her eyes, watch her chin go up, and all the while wanting to reach out and put his arms around her. He'd never expected to find himself feeling this way again. Guilt flashed through him suddenly, over Lora and the justice he hadn't yet gotten for her. Justice he was here to find.

He followed Roxanna through the open doorway that led into the front room of the south wing, and closed the door behind him. The aromas of coffee and beef steak from the kitchen down the hall filled the room.

Roxanna walked ahead through the hall and into the kitchen. Ben stayed where he was.

Hack lounged in his big leather chair, looking comfortable. Ben liked the man, and he wanted Hack to like him as well. Another unsettling feeling. Hack reminded him of the father he'd lost years ago. A man like this could never be Brian Avery, could he? The ranger in him remained cautious. There was too much he didn't know, and there was the money for the Crooked Spur, and that gold watch found on Hack Larabee's man, Rossiter. He couldn't let his loneliness blind him to what might be.

For now, he played his role. "Don't you ever get up?"

Hack grunted. "Don't get smart with me, young fellow. I can whup you real easy."

"I ain't so sure about that."

"I get my hands on you, I'll wring your neck like a chicken."

Ben fought back a smile. "That's a nasty picture you're painting. What am I gonna be doing all that time?"

Hack grinned and got to his feet. Average height, stocky and powerful of build, he yawned and stretched. He had taken off his vest, and the sweat-stained dark blue shirt he wore had fade marks around the shape of the leather.

"With all your money," Ben said, "it seems you could buy a new shirt now and then."

"Your pa ever take you out to the woodshed?"

"Yeah, but it never did much good."

"Maybe it's my turn."

"Too late," Ben said.

Roxanna rang the dinner bell then, so they moved through the hallway and into the kitchen where the table stood near the big iron stove. Supper tasted so delicious, Ben couldn't stop eating. "I could get used to this," he said.

"Well, there sure ain't no leftovers," Hack complained.

Roxanna, sitting at the end of the table, looked a bit more friendly. Ben guessed she was proud of her cooking, even though she pretended not to care what he thought of it.

"Do you have family, Ben?" she asked.

"My father died when I was a kid. My mother's down in Texas. Haven't seen her for a couple of years."

"Do you write her?"

"Whenever I move. She's still young enough to take care of herself, and mean as a razorback, but I like knowing she can reach me if she needs me."

Roxanna eyed him curiously, as if she hadn't thought of him having family feelings. Half amused and half annoyed, he waited for his chance to get back at her a bit.

Later on, she served coffee back in the front room by the crackling fire. She poked at the log with a rod, then warmed her hands. Ben couldn't take his eyes off the glow of her auburn hair in the firelight. He and Hack sat slumped in the leather chairs, and Ben nodded to her as he patted his full stomach.

"That was a tasty meal. So you're good for something after all."

Her nose went up a little. "You do a lot of talking for a man who won't be around very long. The Kendalls will surely bring in someone to cut you down to size. And I for one will be happy to see it."

Ben kept his face straight. "You're just plain mean."

"Is this a game or something? Don't you know somebody's going to be faster than you? You're heading to Boot Hill at a full gallop, and you don't even know it."

Hack grunted. "Roxanna, you could be a little more civil to Ben here." The rancher was clearly having trouble staying awake in his big chair. His eyelids drifted closed and he began to snore with an occasional whistle, which made Roxanna giggle. Then she sobered and poked at the fire again.

After a long silence, she spoke, glancing at the sleeping rancher. "Uncle Hack doesn't like me seeing Miles Kendall."

"That why you're doing it?"

She didn't rise to the bait this time. "I don't know who ordered the killings, but I want to stop it before it gets to my uncle, and seeing Miles might do that."

"Kind of a poor bargain, ain't it?"

She stiffened, chin up. "You don't even know Miles. Obviously I cannot talk to you, Mr. Hawks. You're rude and arrogant."

Fighting not to smile, he said, "Just trying to be like you."

"I can hardly wait to put flowers on your grave."

"I didn't know you cared."

Hands on her hips, she frowned. "You're pushing your luck, Mr. Hawks. I don't want you or any other gunman here. It just escalates the range war."

He considered that for a moment. "Which side are you on?"

She drew a deep breath. "How dare you ask that?"

"Well, you're seeing a Kendall, and I'm here to run them off."

"You lay a hand on Miles, I'll shoot you square between the eyes. And I don't miss."

"I bet you don't."

A smile flickered on her lips, but she fought it off and frowned again, then turned to stoke the fire once more.

He should let things alone, he knew it, but he couldn't. "What about that dandy in town? Chandler Strong."

"Mr. Strong is a gentleman, something you would not understand."

"I saw Gorman. He seemed a little more grounded. And some farmer's kid. Any others knocking on your door?"

"Yes, and it's none of your business."

"I'm here to protect you, remember?"

"I can take care of myself."

"Your uncle deserves some peace around here, which is why he hired me. Besides, you can't go fighting the whole world."

"Just you, Mr. Hawks."

"Yeah, I wondered about that. You've been fighting me so hard since I got here, you must be crazy about me."

She tossed her long tresses with a lift of her chin. Prickly as ever, but there was something new in her dark eyes now, a glint that could be a sign of interest.

Ben got to his feet. "I know you're gonna miss me, but I'm hitting the sack."

He left her by the fireplace, crossed the dog trot, and headed toward his room in the north wing.

Only when the door closed behind Ben did Roxanna realize her uncle had stopped snoring. She turned to look at him. He was smiling as he stretched in his favorite leather chair. "You like Ben, don't you?"

Flustered, she felt a blush rising. "What makes you say that?"

"Because you're afraid of him."

"I'm not afraid of anyone."

"Well, you ain't afraid of Miles. And you sure ain't scared of that dandy, Chandler. Or them others come courting, although I like that Gorman fellow. Not so keen on the farmer. But you don't get rattled when they call, on account of you ain't one bit interested in 'em. Ben, now . . . the minute he came riding up, you got plenty scared. Couldn't stop picking at him. You started falling for him right off, didn't you?"

She grabbed the iron rod and poked at the fire. "I would think you had your fill of men like that."

"The men I rode with were soldiers. Lean and hungry and plumb wore out, and we was lied to, but we were men and we took it. And Ben Hawks can take it. But I ain't so sure about you."

"Uncle Hack, how you go on."

"The truth of the matter is, honey, like me, you're lonely here. Real lonely."

His somber tone made her turn to him again with a smile meant to be reassuring. "I'm not. I have you."

He shook his head. "That's not what I'm talking about."

"So what does a hired gunslinger have to do with who's courting me?"

"All I'm saying is, give the man a chance. You might be surprised."

Later, in her room, she stared into her hand mirror as she combed her long hair. She didn't know if her uncle was right about her being attracted to Ben, but she did feel threatened by him. There was something wild about him, something that conjured up an excitement she'd never felt before, and it terrified her.

She yanked at a knot in her hair. Her uncle was right about

their being lonely, but it had never occurred to her that Uncle Hack needed a woman in his life. She felt guilty that she hadn't considered anyone but herself. What would Uncle Hack do if she agreed to marry Miles? For no good reason, Ben Hawks' face came to mind. Those ice-blue eyes of his that drew her interest, even though she didn't want them to. His very presence rattled her, something she had not experienced until now with any man. She'd heard the stories and the songs, but she hadn't been prepared for that handsome face and the way he seemed to swallow her up with his gaze.

Oh, for Lord's sake. She set her brush on the night-table, climbed into bed, and turned out the lamp. Ben Hawks was rude, arrogant, and likely to get himself killed before long. She was done thinking about him. *For now.*

In his own room, sleep eluded Ben. He couldn't stop thinking about Roxanna. What hope did he have that a woman so gorgeous and spirited would even consider a gunfighter who had wasted three years of his life hunting a man he most likely would never find? Just as no one had ever found his father's killer. *Unless it's Hack I'm after. If it turns out that way, she'll hate me. If it doesn't . . .*

He rolled over on his cot, unable to get comfortable. He had to accept that he could not dictate justice, only pray for it.

CHAPTER EIGHT

In the morning at the Larabee ranch, the sun shone brightly. Ben, arriving for breakfast with the Larabees in the big kitchen, happily stuffed himself with bacon and eggs, big hot biscuits, and thick black coffee.

Hack grinned at him across the table. "You're gonna weigh three hundred pounds in a week."

Roxanna refilled their cups, avoiding Ben's gaze. "You two can clean up the table. I'm going riding."

Hack sobered. "Honey, I don't want you riding alone out there."

"They aren't shooting women these days, Uncle Henry."

"Don't call me Henry. And you listen to me, girl. I got the men riding in pairs, and you ain't no different. Lone riders make a good target. What's more, even if we ain't had no Apaches or Utes come this way, we can't take no chances. They'd sure like to take you along with 'em."

"They'd be real sorry," Ben said. Roxanna glared at him.

Hack chuckled then sobered. "Seriously, Roxanna. Take Buckley with you."

"All right, Uncle Hack."

"Or you can take Ben."

She tossed her head. "I'm sure you'll be busy with Mr. Hawks all day. And I want to go to the ridge."

"Just be sure to take Buckley," Hack snapped.

"Okay," she said, chin up. "But I'm a better shot than he is."

"Just don't tell him that," Hack said.

She smiled at Hack's joke, turned, and left the room.

Ben shifted in his chair. "What's the ridge?"

"High point in the valley. You can see for miles. She likes the trees turning color."

Ben grabbed another biscuit. "I ran into a cavalry patrol on my way up from Mesilla. They said some Indian war bands were on the move, but they're like ghosts."

"Now you mention it, we'll just take a ride out toward the ridge ourselves. Buckley's a good kid but he's no fighter."

"Yeah, sure, soon as I finish."

Hack chuckled. "You act like you haven't eaten in years."

"I don't think I have," Ben said, reaching for the jam. He slopped some on the hot biscuit and took a generous bite.

When Hack and Ben walked outside, the sun shone bright in a clear sky of eggshell blue. No wind, but it still felt cold and damp. Hack led the way down the slope toward the corrals. Three men were breaking a horse near the barn. One of them mounted, and flew right up into the air as the horse bucked. The unlucky rider landed on the fence with a yell and a crash. The other men laughed as he got up and shook himself off. The door of the bunkhouse nearby stood open, and a steady stream of smoke rose from the chimney of the cookhouse next to it. Ben felt at home, a strange feeling considering his purpose here.

"Got me near thirty hands, all told," Hack said. "Half of 'em are out on the range or at the line shacks. But you're my first gunfighter. If that's what you want to call yourself."

Ben shook his head, and pushed his hat back to enjoy the sun on his face. He wondered if any of those thirty ranch hands were—or had been—outlaw riders with Brian Avery.

Sloan, grumpy-looking as ever, came out of the bunkhouse. As they walked toward him, Sloan's eyes narrowed, but when

Hack introduced Ben as a new hire, he acted friendly enough. "Heard you shot the Pecos Kid," Sloan said as he adjusted his hat.

Ben nodded.

"Pretty tight-lipped about it, huh?" Sloan shrugged. "You working for us, or just walking around looking pretty?"

"He's just working personal for me and Roxanna," Hack said. "And watching our backs."

Sloan nodded, his respect for Hack clear in his face.

"You got enough hands," Hack added.

"Yes, sir," Sloan said, and turned away.

Alone with Ben once more, Hack grinned. "Sloan's an old timer and rides for the brand. You can trust him with your life."

Later, saddling up by the corral to ride with Hack into the wooded hills, Ben enjoyed the rancher's admiration of his chestnut gelding.

"Holy smoke, Ben. Where did you get him?"

"San Antonio. Bought him as a colt. Good blood lines, but he had a bad right foreleg, and they were gonna shoot 'im. I took him and nursed him out of it."

Hack folded his arms and leaned on the fence post. "I'd give my eye teeth for a horse like that. Gentle, ain't he? By golly, Ben, I'd sure like to buy 'im."

"He ain't for sale."

Hack grinned. "No, I guess not. Let's head north, and I'll show you how big we are. We need more grass. Tried to buy the Lazy K when a Yank owned it, but he sold it to the Kendalls 'count of they were from Boston. So I tried to buy it from them, and they tried to buy me out. We stopped the dickering when Laird Kendall got bushwhacked."

"Why don't you just drive some of your cattle to the railhead and spread yourself thinner?"

"Because I'm a stubborn old fool."

They swung up and started off. Ben kept quiet, busy with his own thoughts. He liked Hack more than made him comfortable, still unsure how Hack, just out of prison back in '74, had gotten enough money to buy a place like this. He told himself to relax and enjoy the day, if he could.

They rode north through the valley near rolling hills and canyons lined with juniper, pinyon pine, and scrub oak. A right pretty land, it glistened with all-year creeks amid the tall grass. Thousands of head of cattle grazed everywhere. On occasion, riders waved at Ben and Hack as they passed by. Ben envied Hack, who seemed to have everything a man could want.

Later, as they rested in the shade of a cottonwood near a crystal-clear stream about a mile or two from the ridge, Hack lay on the grass with his hat over his eyes. He didn't look like a hard-riding major from the Confederate army, nor like an outlaw who had outwitted his trackers for years. Nor did he seem like the kind of brutal man Brian Avery had to be, yet Ben remained careful. He'd known this man less than two days, after all.

He sat near the rancher. "Heard you raised a ruckus after the war."

Hack kept his hat over his eyes as he answered. "Yeah, well, I was younger then. My brother died in my arms in prison, and that's when I realized I was wasting my life on something I couldn't do nothing about. That's plenty hard for a man to live with. And then my brother's wife died right after I got a pardon. So I took Roxanna in and brought her out here."

"Seems you got a good life."

Silence fell between them. Then Hack spoke. "You're thinking like a lawman, Ben. I can tell. You're wondering where I got the money for this spread."

A chill threaded up Ben's spine. Damn, the man was quick.

"I guess you're right."

Hack's hat still obscured his face. "When we were the only ones denied amnesty after the war, my brother and I got plenty mad. We decided we were done cooperating. And that's all I got to say on the subject. But I was sure glad to get out of that rat hole."

"Grant did you a good turn."

"Grant knew what it was like to be a soldier."

Hack lay quiet as if dozing. The sun warmed them and the stream sparkled and danced. Ben wanted to ask more about Hack's prison time and its aftermath, but knew he'd get nowhere right now. He set the subject aside and looked around with pleasure. "It's one of the nicest spreads I've ever seen."

"It's a good one, yes. And a good place to be. Except for the Lazy K."

They fell silent again, this time for a long while. It dawned on Ben that he liked this man and respected him, no matter what his past. He didn't want to believe Hack Larabee and Brian Avery were the same person. He wanted to trust his own instincts. But as Hack had said, he couldn't stop being a lawman.

He tossed a rock at the creek. "Who found Rossiter's body?"

"Sloan and one of the boys. It wasn't long after Laird Kendall got shot dead over on the Lazy K. We figure they were getting even."

"You don't figure one of your own boys shot Laird Kendall?"

"Not likely, and if they did, it sure weren't on my orders." Hack swept the hat off his face and sat up. "And now I figure the Lazy K will try picking us off one at a time. They think they can force me to sell, and I'm not about to do that."

"What did you know about Rossiter before you hired him on?"

"Not a thing. Just another hand riding the grub line."

Ben sat quiet, staring at the stream.

"Tell me something, Ben," Hack said after a while. "Why'd you join the rangers?"

"My pa was a deputy sheriff, got shot when I was ten, and they never found out who bushwhacked him. I reckon I just wanted to be like him. Wore a badge as soon as I was old enough, and then the rangers called on me."

Hack went quiet for a long time, turning his hat in his hands. "I lost my folks before the war. My wife died while I was in it, and then my son got it at Franklin. He was a foot soldier. With another outfit. I didn't even know he'd joined up. He was too young for it."

In his voice as much as the words, Ben heard loneliness. Clearly, Hack's family had meant a lot to him. Roxanna surely did. Ben had seen that himself. He stared off into the distance. Loneliness was something he knew too well. He'd let the rangers be his guide in life, but even at thirty, he missed his father. He felt a kinship of sorts with Hack right now, despite the question of Hack's identity that held him back.

Silently, Ben prayed that Hack Larabee had no connection with Avery.

A critter rustled in the nearby brush. The sun cast warmth and shadows. Finally, Hack spoke. "What do you think of Roxanna?"

Ben grinned. "She's a kick."

Hack grinned back. "She's got more fire in her than most men."

Ben didn't answer.

Hack persisted. "You like her?"

"If I did, would you run me off?"

Hack chuckled. "Think I could?"

"Nope." The enjoyment of joking with Hack ebbed as Ben recalled his circumstances. Truth was, he didn't consider himself worthy of a beautiful, spirited woman like Roxanna. He'd been too long on a trail of vengeance that left him eaten up inside.

Hack settled his hat on his head. "I came out of prison a bitter man," he said. "Roxanna gave me back my life. She could do the same for the right fellow."

Did Hack mean him? Surely not. They sat gazing at the sparkling water as it danced downward over the rocks.

A red-headed, black buzzard appeared in the blue sky. Hack nodded toward it. "He's back again." The buzzard sailed over the ridge to the west, where it disappeared.

Shots rang out from the north on the faraway red-streaked ridge where the junipers gave way to rocks and brush. Hack paled. "That's where Roxanna and Buckley went."

They got to their feet in a hurry.

CHAPTER NINE

Moving fast, Ben and Hack cut through the trees and up a long gully, then came out on a rise a good mile from the rocky ridge that rose beyond the rolling grassland like a fortress.

Hack pulled his rifle from its scabbard. "Don't see nothing. She likes to get up there to look at the valley. There's a trail runs up behind it and circles the top. Only thing this side is a deer path, steep, winds up around the front of it." He eyed Ben. "You're younger than me. I'll take the trail in back, you head up this side."

Ben nodded. "Let's go."

They separated, Hack following the gully to circle toward the back of the ridge.

Ben moved through the pines and wiry brush to his right, sweat on his face as much from worry as from the hot sun. Anyone laid a hand on Roxanna, they'd be real sorry. He urged his chestnut at a gallop through the trees toward the winding deer path.

Shots rang out again from the ridge, and he dug in his heels. His horse responded despite the dangerous path through trees, rocks, and brush. Ben had long ago lost sight of Hack. Hopefully the rancher had already moved out of the gully and up the trail on the other side.

Partway up the deer path, Ben reined in his horse and reached down to quiet the animal. Another shot echoed from the ridge. He drew his Winchester repeater, wondering if Hack had taken that bullet. Better to assume Roxanna and Buckley were putting up a fight against their attackers.

The trail was too narrow for the chestnut, the grade too steep. Ben dismounted, and headed on foot up the path, his boots slipping and sliding in the dirt and loose rocks. Around eight hundred feet up, about a third of the way, he paused to catch his breath. More shots echoed up ahead, and he started forward again. Earth sliding under his boots, the trail getting steeper, Ben was soon a hundred feet from the top. From the sounds of the gunfire, someone on higher terrain at the back of the ridge had someone else pinned down in the rocks on Ben's side.

Sweating heavily, he reached the rim of the ridge and saw a sorrel horse and a bay standing off behind some boulders to his right. He climbed a little more and spied a heavy-set man in front of him, lying on his belly between two large rocks and firing his rifle up at a higher rise. The man's cohort had to be firing from another hiding place on the other side of the trail. But someone above had this fellow pinned down. Hack? Ben had no idea if the rancher had made it that far.

The big man in front of Ben cocked his repeater and tried to slide out from between the rocks. Bullets spattered around him, holding him in position again.

Ben ducked behind some nearby rocks for protection. Was he safe showing himself? Roxanna or Buckley could pick him off if they didn't know who he was. He took off his hat and waved it above the rocks, hoping that would do the trick. Then he put his hat back on and rose with his Winchester trained on the bushwhacker in front of him. "Drop that rifle."

The heavy-set man rolled over and froze. Ben's rifle barrel poked at his big belly. With a square face and flat nose, the man looked plenty mean. He tossed his rifle aside. *Mean but not stupid*, Ben thought. He poked the fellow again. "Now the six-gun, way out."

Scowling, the big man sent his Colt sliding down the slope, its barrel catching dirt. His rifle rested a few feet from his reach, but he didn't go for it.

Ben poked him a third time, gesturing for him to roll on his belly. The man obeyed.

Another shot rang out from above. Ben's hat went flying. He jumped behind a rock near the prone bushwhacker. "It's me, blast it," he shouted. "I got him, so hold off!"

The man lunged for his rifle, rolled over, and fired. The bullet grazed the left side of Ben's head, burning his skin and knocking him back. His Winchester went flying. He landed on his rear and his head hit the rock. Stunned, he struggled to rise before his attacker could shoot again.

The bushwhacker's rifle jammed. He leaped up and charged. He landed hard on Ben and rolled with him down out of the rocks. Ben felt the power of the man's big hands, the heavy weight of his body as they crashed against a boulder.

Ben slammed his fist in the man's face. His attacker fell backward. Ben rose to his knees, then staggered to his feet as the bushwhacker did the same. The big man's nose bled, and his eyes looked wild. His six-gun lay in the dirt some twenty feet away. His own rifle was back in the rocks. Ben eyed the bushwhacker, weighing his odds. He still had his own six-guns, looped in their holsters. How fast could he draw?

"I'll break you in half," the big man snarled.

Ben reached for his righthand six-gun. The whole world crashed into him from behind, knocking him down and crushing him like a bug. He fought for a glimpse of his new assailant, caught a swift impression of a huge, bearded man on top of him, pummeling him with ham-sized fists. Fighting furiously to get free, Ben sensed the other bushwhacker jumping into the fray. He squirmed out from under both attackers as the huge man hit the other's bleeding nose. The first bushwhacker yelped in pain.

As Ben got to one knee, both bushwhackers fell on him again, slamming into him like huge boulders. He tried to roll out from under, but the heavier man's knee pressed the side of his neck. He couldn't budge, could hardly breathe.

A voice rang out from nearby rocks. "Hold it!" Hack bellowed. "Or I'll blow your teeth plumb out."

Ben squirmed free as his attackers got off of him. Gasping for air, he sat up and wiped dirt from his mouth. He was drenched with sweat and felt as if he'd been caught in a stampede. Blood trickled down the side of his head as he looked up at Hack. "About time you got here."

Hack grinned. "You was doing all right."

Ben got to his feet, wincing. He took the bigger bushwhacker's six-gun and made both of them lie on their bellies. While Hack tied their hands behind their backs with rawhide strings from their saddles, Ben washed the wound on his head with water from Hack's canteen. The bleeding had stopped, so he didn't bind it. He retrieved his hat, shaking his head at the bullet hole in the crown.

"These boys work for the Kendalls," Hack said. "The biggest one's called Pinkley. The fellah with the flat nose, that's Posher." He glared at the gunmen. "Now what were you boys shooting at?"

"We saw a buck," Posher snarled.

"And it was shooting back at you?" Hack demanded.

Beyond Hack, Ben looked up to see Roxanna, rifle in hand, standing on the rough terrain far above. She wore riding skirts with a heavy dark blue jacket, her hat thrown back and her silken hair blowing in the breeze. She waved frantically at them.

Hack waved back. "Go on, Ben. I'll watch these varmints."

Ben started up the slope. Dirty and sweaty and plumb wore

out already, he struggled through brush and rocks to the rise where she waited. Her dark brown eyes were brimming with tears even as she held her rifle ready.

"They shot Buckley," she said when Ben reached her. "I did what I could for him, but he needs help."

Ben moved around her toward where the young ranch hand lay on his right side amid the rocks. He knelt by the wounded Buckley, noting blood on his shirt and a hastily tied bandanna behind the left shoulder.

"We'd just come up here, and they was waiting for us," Buckley said through clenched teeth. The freckles across his cheeks stood out against his pallor. "As soon as we hit the skyline, they fired. I was the target. They didn't try to shoot Miss Roxanna." He flicked a glance toward her and tried to smile. "Except she really gave 'em what for."

Ben undid the bandanna and pulled Buckley's shirt open. "Get a canteen. And a clean cloth if you have it."

She hurried to where the horses waited on the back trail and returned with a clothbound canteen and a fresh bandanna. Ben washed and covered the wound. Buckley winced with every touch.

"Bullet just grazed you," Ben said as he helped the cowhand sit up. The boy's temple was bruised and scraped, but it didn't look too bad.

"Yeah, but I whacked my head on those rocks when I fell. Missed most of the gunfight, I guess."

"Can you ride?"

"I think so."

Ben's flesh wound stung, but it would heal. He stood up, hat in hand, and poked his finger through the bullet hole in the crown. "Well, if you was out," he said, "then I reckon I know who nearly killed me."

When he turned to look at Roxanna, her cheeks were flushed

but her chin rose in the air as she fought to maintain her composure. "You're lucky," she said. "I didn't account for the elevation."

Ben almost smiled as he set his hat back on. He waved down to Hack, signaling not to worry. When he looked back at Roxanna, she was sitting on a rock, cradling her rifle in her arms and fighting tears. He laid a hand on her shoulder and squeezed gently. She was trembling, which surprised him. She drew the back of her hand across her eyes but didn't move or shake his hand away.

"You did all right," he said.

"I could have killed you," she whispered.

"I thought that was the idea."

She looked up, shock and anger in her face. Then she saw the twinkle in his eye and gave a shaky smile. "You have a weird sense of humor," she said.

"I got no other way to handle you."

She struggled to her feet, glaring at him again. Then, as if realizing he'd riled her on purpose to bring her back to life, she began to laugh while wiping away her tears. She looked at Buckley, who was smiling now, then downhill to Hack, who seemed to have caught the drift of the conversation. Hack grinned at them all and waved.

They headed back through the valley to the Larabee ranch with the prisoners and Buckley, who went to see the cook and get patched up. Instead of dismounting, Roxanna abruptly turned her horse and rode off toward the eastern hills. Hack grimaced, watching her disappear into the woods.

"She's gone to the pond," he told Ben. "We'll be headed for town soon's we get Buckley patched up and the prisoners ready. You can catch up with us later."

Ben shrugged, adjusted the cinch on his saddle, and swung astride.

Roxanna rode into the woods with tears brimming in her eyes. She'd nearly shot Ben on the ridge, and as much as she wanted to dislike him, she found it difficult. What was Ben Hawks to her, anyway? A hired gunslinger who probably wanted to die. Why should she be this upset over nearly shooting him, when she hadn't actually done it?

She made her way through aspens and oaks into the clearing where the creek had spread into a large, deep pond. She'd been here swimming many times. Under the warm sun, she dismounted and sat on a rock. Her roan nudged her back, as it often did, then lowered its head and began to graze. She watched it awhile, then gazed at the pond, and gradually felt calmer.

A twig cracked behind her, and her horse lifted its head. She turned and saw Ben, who'd quietly ridden up and now sat on horseback some fifty feet away.

She stood hastily and glared at him. The last thing she wanted was for him to know how badly shaken she was by what happened at the ridge, and how much remorse she still felt.

Ben dismounted, dropped the reins, and came over to her. "I didn't ask you to follow me," she snapped.

He pushed his hat back from his brow. "You're a lot of trouble."

"My uncle needs your help. I don't."

She sat again on the rock. Ben came to stand near her and looked out over the deep pond.

"Go away," she said.

Her horse came up and nudged her again as Ben walked to the edge of the water, then squatted on his heels. Roxanna's horse ambled up behind him. She knew what was coming, and bit her lip to keep back laughter as the horse set its nose on Ben's rear and nudged hard.

Caught off balance, Ben staggered and fell into the water with a loud splash. He got to his feet and stood hip deep as he retrieved his hat and hoisted his gun belt out of the wet. He looked so rattled, she felt an unexpected wave of affection. She started laughing so hard, she couldn't stop.

Ben climbed out of the water, hat dripping, boots squishing. He removed his Colts and sat on a rock near where she stood. He pulled off his boots, dumped the water out, shook them, and yanked them back on. He wasn't smiling, but he didn't look angry or embarrassed, either.

Roxanna finally stopped laughing and wiped tears from her eyes. She sat down next to him, stifling another laugh as she pushed her nudging horse away. Then she tugged a handkerchief from her belt and handed it over. "Here."

He gave it a skeptical glance, but took it anyway. "Won't do much good, but thanks."

She watched him wipe down his Colts and then his hair, and set his soaked hat back on his head. She couldn't help admiring how calm he was, taking in stride his unplanned dip in the pond. Sobering, she clasped her hands together and stared into the water.

"I could have killed you," she said.

"You're a lousy shot."

Angered, she moved to stand, then saw his half-smile and sat back down. "My uncle needs you. Go on back."

"Not without you."

Drawing a deep breath, she nodded and stood. Ben got to his feet and handed her the handkerchief. She folded the damp fabric while he buckled his Colts back on. She waited for him to smile at her again, but he turned and headed for his horse without so much as a look at her. For a brief moment, she wanted to go to him and demand his attention, maybe even a hug, but he had already mounted.

Disappointed for no reason that made sense, she mounted and rode up beside him. His clothes were soaked. She remembered his look of surprise as he flopped into the water.

He met her gaze just as she giggled, and rode on ahead.

Back at the ranch, Roxanna dismounted and gave her horse to one of the hands. Ignoring Hack's glare, she hurried over to the house and went inside.

Hack noted Ben's wet clothes, grinned, and turned to the business at hand. "Let's get these fellows into town. You'll dry off on the way."

With Pinkley and Posher in tow, they arrived in town at twilight. Reilly greeted them with a raised eyebrow. "Things heating up out there? What'd these fellows do?"

Hack handed over the prisoners. "Shot at my niece. Wounded one of my ranch hands, but not bad. He's mending." He glanced at Ben. "You should see the doc for that head graze."

"I'm all right," Ben said, but went anyway when Reilly added his voice to Hack's. The doctor's wide-eyed look when Ben arrived at his office made it clear the man remembered the gunfight with the Pecos Kid, but he looked Ben over competently enough and cleared him. Ben thought about explaining himself, but weariness overcame him and he decided against it. He headed back toward the jailhouse with a sense of relief.

At the marshal's office later that night, with the two hired guns locked in a back cell behind the closed wooden door, Hack and Ben sat around the hot, smoky iron stove and drank coffee with the lawman.

"Good thing you have a hard head," Hack told Ben.

Reilly grinned. "I told you Hack's niece was a heck of a shot."

"She aimed too high," Hack mused.

"Maybe on purpose," Reilly said. "I mean, she must find Ben kind of lovable."

Ben couldn't enjoy the banter. His head was pounding. He slouched in his chair, sipped his coffee, and made a face. "This stuff could kill a snake."

"If you were sitting on a stove in a tin pot all day long, you'd be the same," Reilly said with a grin. "Don't worry on it. That stuff will make a man of you."

"Truth is," Hack said to Ben, "he just keeps adding grounds to the old brew."

Ben set his cup aside and briefly closed his eyes. Dark and cold outside, but plenty warm inside. For the first time since the gunfight up on the ridge, he allowed himself to relax. "So what happens next with Pinkley and Posher?"

Reilly gulped coffee. "We'd never get 'em to Lincoln or Mesilla for trial, not with the Lazy K worried what they're gonna say. We'd better wait for the circuit judge. He oughta be here next week."

Hack scowled. "That gives Kendall time to get some fancy lawyer."

Ben leaned back in his chair. "Don't matter. I caught 'em dead to rights, and I can testify."

"If you're still around," Reilly said.

"If we head back to my place, are you gonna be all right here?" Hack asked the lawman.

Reilly nodded. "I'll sign up some deputies, and this place is like a fortress."

Two days later, over breakfast at the Larabee ranch house, Hack brought up Roxanna. She'd been avoiding their company, likely because she was still embarrassed over shooting at Ben. "I think she likes you," Hack said.

"Yeah, that's why she missed."

Hack grinned but sobered when Roxanna walked into the kitchen with Miles Kendall. Miles wore ranch clothes under a long coat. He had a fancy new hat, a blue vest, and a single sidearm. Roxanna took his coat and hat and hung them on a wall hook.

"Ben Hawks, this is Miles Kendall," Roxanna said, her cheeks dark with color as she briefly met Ben's gaze

Ben didn't rise or offer his hand. He sized Miles up, noting that the man kept his distance. An easterner in western clothes, not someone who belonged out here. He could tell that, and wondered why Roxanna apparently couldn't. What was she doing with this dandy, who wasn't a patch on the kind of man she needed?

Hack half rose out of his chair. Roxanna hurried to him and laid her hand on his shoulder. "Uncle Hack, Miles had nothing to do with the attack on the ridge."

"I would never let any harm come to her," Miles said. Ben bristled at the man's possessive tone. He talked like Roxanna was already his.

Roxanna seated Miles between herself and her uncle. Ben sat alone at the end of the table. The eggs and bacon, tasty a minute ago, lost their savor as he watched Roxanna fix Miles Kendall a plate and then start making more coffee at the stove.

As they ate, Miles glanced at Roxanna, admiration clear in his face. Then he turned to Ben with a frown. "I hear you shot the Pecos Kid."

Hack grimaced. "Ben refused to be another notch on his gun. You got any idea who Pecos was working for?"

Miles shook his head. "No, but I also heard you have two of our men in jail."

"They tried to bushwhack Buckley, and he was riding with my niece."

"I had no hand in it," Miles said. "And they will be fired."

"They'll be doing time," Hack said.

Roxanna turned slowly from the stove. "Miles didn't know."

"That's right," Miles said to her. "Now, what about our ride?"

She smiled at him. "Have your breakfast first."

Irritated, Ben held out his cup for a refill. Roxanna obliged but avoided his gaze. Miles looked surprised at their silent exchange.

"Roxanna took a shot at Ben up on the ridge," Hack said.

"A lady sharpshooter?" Miles asked, humor in his voice.

She stiffened. "I thought he was one of them. And I missed."

Miles' grin widened. "Remind me to be careful."

After Roxanna and her visitor left the breakfast table, Hack downed the rest of his coffee in anger. "I don't know what she sees in him," Hack growled.

Ben shrugged. His own agitation made no sense to him. Roxanna wasn't likely to walk out with him, a hired gunslinger, with a range war brewing. "Ain't no figuring a woman."

Hack stared into his cup. "I don't trust Kendall, but I don't reckon he'd ever put Roxanna in danger. He wants her along with our spread."

"He's a real dude, and I agree he'd not want her hurt, but however it happened, or whoever paid for it, there's no denying those two gunmen work for the Lazy K," Ben said.

"Maybe he'll let 'em face up to it in court, without no fancy lawyer."

"No matter who's behind what happened yesterday, they'll worry Pinkley and Posher'll talk to save their necks."

Hack sighed. "Which means they either got to bust 'em out or kill 'em."

A moment of silence fell. Ben couldn't stop thinking of Roxanna and Miles Kendall, out there alone in the sunshine. The beautiful girl and the handsome, rich dude with his fine manners and speech.

"You want me to follow your niece?" Ben asked.

"I sure do."

Roxanna rode at Miles' side, crossing the valley under a clear sky. He talked about his last visit to St. Louis and all the fine and wonderful things he had seen, but she barely heard the details. As they rode, she stared off at the distant herd. Until now, she'd been content to allow Miles to come calling. She'd even thought about marrying him, if it would keep the peace. After all, he was educated, pleasant, and had good manners. How much better could she do out here?

But meeting Ben had knocked her off balance, and she didn't know what she wanted anymore. Introducing Miles to him back at the ranch had made her feel disloyal, an odd sensation. She would be devastated if Ben disliked her or considered her fickle, and wasn't that a crazy thing to realize? What was the matter with her?

"Miss Roxanna, you aren't listening."

She recovered swiftly. "I was just wishing the killing would stop."

"I didn't know what those two men were up to, I promise you. And I don't know who killed my brother or your man Rossiter. Maybe someone else is trying to start a range war between the Lazy K and the Crooked Spur, ever think of that?"

"And they paid your men to do it?"

"Anything's possible."

"I'm sorry, Miles. I'm spoiling your visit." But as they rode down to the canyon where a little creek ran busily along, its water sparkling in the sunshine, so many questions tumbled through her mind that she couldn't revive her smile if she'd tried.

They reined up near the creek, and Roxanna took a moment

to enjoy its music. "How's Vera?" she asked.

"Still grieving for my brother."

"It's been six months. I should go see her."

"She keeps to herself. Let it be for now."

Roxanna sighed. "I guess that's best. She never liked me anyway."

Miles grinned. "Do women ever like someone who's younger and prettier?"

He was good at compliments. She smiled her thanks.

They dismounted, her roan nosing her back and pushing until she turned to pet it. Miles spread a blanket on the damp grass. He grinned at the sight of her Winchester in her hand. "Is that for me?"

"Just habit," she said. She looked around at the thick stands of brush, still heavy with white flowers, on both sides of the creek. Then she glanced down at the soft red earth near the water. "Look. Don't you see those tracks?"

He looked where she pointed. "A white-tail deer, that's all."

"Not those." She gestured to several sets of small, weaving prints. "Over there."

"Just some critters had a little too much rye."

She laughed. "Skunk."

He grinned. "You think they'll be back?"

"Yes, and they don't care if we're in the way or not."

"So I'm with a real animal tracker." He scooped up the blanket and draped it over one arm. They led their mounts further up the creek and stopped near a huge cottonwood, its narrow leaves yellowed. Beneath it lay sweet grass. Across the stream, the terrain rose rapidly into high rocks, and pinyon pines stood dark against golden aspens. Above the timber, the rocky terrain rose to the sunny sky.

He spread the blanket in the shade of the cottonwood. She sat near him as he removed his hat and lay back, his hands behind his head. He still wore his revolver. Some unseen varmint played in the brush behind and to their right, past the big tree. With the horses ground-tied nearby, it all seemed mighty safe and peaceful, as if there was no range war.

She set down her Winchester at the edge of the blanket, removed her hat, and rested on her elbow. Miles caught her eye. "Miss Roxanna, you know I'm crazy about you."

"My uncle's not crazy about you."

"It's just the Kendall name. Tell you what. I'll change it."

She laughed softly. "It's not that easy."

"Then tell me how to win him over."

"Miles, he's a stubborn man. This is his country, and you and your brother moved in on him."

"We bought our ranch from a legitimate owner."

"Who refused to sell to my uncle," she said. "Because he wore gray."

"If you marry me, we could put the ranches together."

"And Vera?"

"I can buy her out."

"Let's not talk about anything serious, Miles. It's too beautiful a day."

She lay down on the blanket near him and stared up at the clear sky through the leaves of the cottonwood. She wished it could always be this peaceful. Up in the higher branches, a bluebird, its gray belly streaked, fluttered its annoyance and flew away. Shortly thereafter, its smaller lady friend followed. Roxanna watched them out of sight. Then she glanced over and watched a striped chipmunk in the rocks across the stream. It rose up on its hind legs, studied her, then quickly disappeared.

A gentle tug on her hair startled her. Miles had risen on his elbow and was twirling her long auburn tresses with his fingers. She wondered frantically if she had misled him a little too much.

She drew away from his touch and sat up. He frowned.

"Roxanna, you must know I'm in love with you."

"Miles, please don't."

"Marry me."

She got to her feet. He stood up, pushing his hat back, an uncertain look on his face.

"Don't you remember my father died in prison?" she asked. "And my uncle and he were both outlaws after the war?"

He came close to her. "Why should that matter?"

"It mattered to me," she said. "While they were robbing banks, I was kicked out of finishing school. I ended up being shunned. In fact, I even shunned myself."

"But you were innocent."

"Don't get me wrong, Miles. I wasn't ashamed of my father or my uncle because they went bad after the war. I know why they kept on fighting. But I was selfish when I convinced them to accept amnesty."

"Sounds like you were just trying to keep them alive."

"They were denied amnesty and sent to prison. And I blame myself because I asked them to give themselves up."

He took her gently by the shoulders. "Roxanna, nothing you could have said would have influenced them one way or another about amnesty. I'm sure they listened to you, but they were grown men and made their own decisions. So stop thinking a young girl in finishing school changed anything."

She dabbed at her wet eyes. "Thank you, Miles. But I know what people think and say about my family, behind my back."

"I don't care what they say."

"Miles, your family is rich and prominent."

"But they're in Boston, and I'm out here, with you."

"I don't think they'd want me. They might even disown you."

He took her hands in his. "Roxanna, I'm rich in my own right. And we could have a real life together."

A rifle cracked from the boulders high above the creek. Miles jerked, and she saw blood on his right shoulder. He shoved her aside and pulled his six-gun. The horses snorted and danced away as far as their ties would let them.

Two more shots rang out, hitting Miles in the thigh and chest. Roxanna caught up her Winchester as Miles grunted and dropped to his knees. He crawled toward cover behind the trunk of the cottonwood, Roxanna right beside him. When they reached the tree, Miles struggled partway up, raising his pistol to fire at their unseen foes. Another bullet struck him in mid-chest. He fell back in a heap.

Frantic, she cocked her Winchester repeater and waited, standing behind the tree until one of the two attackers rose up from the rocks. Miles fought to get to his knees again, blood soaking his shirt and vest. The gunman fired as Roxanna stepped out and fired back. His shot hit Miles. Her own shot sent the gunslinger into a jerking spin, and he fell out of sight.

She cocked another shell in the chamber as she hovered behind the cottonwood. The second gunman kept out of sight.

She lowered her Winchester, eased backward, and knelt by Miles. He didn't move, didn't seem to be breathing.

Tears in her eyes, she whispered a frantic prayer.

CHAPTER TEN

Riding out after Miles and Roxanna, Ben grumbled to himself. She didn't belong with a dandy like Kendall. With her wild spirit, she needed to be as free as that old turkey buzzard hovering far away in the blue sky. Frustrated, he tugged at his hat brim. It would never set well, being her bodyguard, trying to keep his distance and biting back words he had no right to say.

Sudden gunfire cracked out from over the next barren hill, the way Roxanna and Miles had gone. Ben kicked his horse to a gallop, hunched in the saddle and ready to draw.

As he rounded the hill, he saw the creek and the giant cottonwood. On the far side, amid a tumble of rocks and trees, a man's body lay sprawled near a fallen rifle. Roxanna knelt by Miles, who lay still in the grass. Disturbing as Ben found that sight, his heart gladdened when she rose from Miles' side, turned, and lifted a hand.

From high up in the rocks and trees, another gunman rose and fired at Ben, then dropped out of sight. The bullet scorched Ben's skin on his left side. Swearing at the pain, he spotted the gunman mounting his horse to ride away under cover in the high woods.

Ben reined up, pulled his rifle, and cocked it. He barely had time to aim before he fired. His shot echoed loud and clear.

The escaping assailant jerked in the saddle, one arm flying upward, then fell from his mount and landed between a large rock and a pine. His sprawled-out legs, the only part of him still visible, stayed completely still. Ben saw no further movement, except for the man's horse trotting off amid the trees.

Roxanna straightened as Ben dismounted and came over. "I think it's too late," she whispered as he knelt by Miles' body and felt for a neck pulse. From the east came rapid hoofbeats. Ben tensed, ready for more trouble, then relaxed as he recognized Sloan and several ranch hands approaching. Clearly shaken, Roxanna leaned her rifle on the cottonwood.

Ben stood as Sloan and the hands reined up. "Two men up there in the trees," Ben said. "Both dead."

Sloan dismounted. "We saw it." He sent four of the hands off to recover the dead gunmen. "What about Kendall?"

Silently, Ben shook his head.

Roxanna stared down at Miles. Ben touched her arm. She turned and pressed against him with a sob. Not knowing what else to do, he held her until she straightened and moved away, hugging herself. He wanted to say something, anything, but his voice caught in his throat. Only now did he realize how much seeing her in danger had terrified him.

"Miss Roxanna," Sloan said, "you did what you had to do."

She looked at the foreman blankly. Then her gaze sharpened. "Ben, you're bleeding."

"Just a scratch. He wasn't near as good a shot as you."

Roxanna half smiled, then grew tearful again. She blinked hard a few times, and Ben had the feeling she was making herself watch as Sloan and the remaining hands laid Miles across his saddle, tied him down, and covered him with a blanket. As three of the hands headed back to the ranch with the dead man, Sloan asked, "You all right, Miss Roxanna?"

She nodded and followed his gaze uphill as the other four hands came down, leading two more horses with bodies across the saddles.

Sloan eyed the two dead men. "Not from Kendall's bunch."

"I know one," Ben said. "A hired gun from Texas."

Sloan helped the shaken Roxanna mount her roan. She looked ready to cry again. Slowly, she turned her horse and followed the men with the dead.

Sloan looked at Ben. "We heard the shots but couldn't get here in time. I'm glad you did."

"They weren't after her," Ben said. "But why kill Miles?"

"Something we ain't got figured as yet."

They turned to their horses and mounted up.

Back at the Larabee ranch, Hack came outside as Ben and the other riders reached the corral in rising wind. Storm clouds darkened the sky and rain threatened.

Ben and Roxanna dismounted. The bullet graze under Ben's arm still hurt, but he ignored it. Sloan tied Kendall's horse, with the rancher's body on it, to the corral fence while two of the hands headed to the barn for the wagon. The dead gunmen lay tied across their own saddles, uncovered against the elements.

Hack hurried over. Roxanna fell into his embrace. Ben wiped sweat from his brow with the back of his hand as Sloan walked over to them.

"Miles Kendall's dead," Sloan said. "Other two are hired guns we never saw before. Miss Roxanna got one of them. She was trying to save Kendall."

Hack hugged Roxanna a little tighter as Sloan continued. "Hawks got the other with an impossible shot." The foreman sounded admiring, which Ben accepted with a shrug. He'd only done what he had to do.

"Can't prove yet who hired 'em," Sloan added. "But Hawks recognized one, said he was a hired gun from Texas." Sloan scratched his scalp beneath his hat. "It don't make no sense. Maybe it's not the Lazy K causing all the trouble. Maybe it's some outsider. Otherwise, why kill Miles Kendall?"

The same question had occurred to Ben. He thought it over as the two ranch hands came forward with a team of sorrels and the wagon, and Hack directed them to take the dead men to town. It could be Avery making trouble, assuming Hack wasn't him. But why? And if Hack wasn't the infamous outlaw, who was?

A light rain began to fall. Sloan and his men loaded the bodies on the wagon. As Ben moved to help, his arm wound stung again. He winced, and Hack glanced toward him. "Get over to the cook," Hack said. "He's as good a doctor as we have around here. Then come join us."

Hack led Roxanna inside, and Ben went over to the cookhouse. Burly and sweating, the cook washed the injury. "Just a crease," he told Ben. "But it's gonna hurt bad for a while. Keep it clean, and if it gets all red, see the doctor."

The cook poured liquid on the cut, and Ben yelped. "What was that?"

The cook grinned. "Horse liniment. Good for what ails ya." He wrapped a clean bandanna around Ben's left arm, then helped Ben put his shirt, coat, and hat back on.

The rain was falling harder now. Wearily, Ben walked up to the ranch house, grimacing whenever his left arm moved. *That horse liniment made it worse.* He stopped in the storeroom where he slept and changed to a clean shirt. The effort started him bleeding again, but he shoved a clean bandanna under the one tied in place. He pulled his coat and hat on, quickly washed his hands in the china bowl he'd been given, then left his room.

As he crossed under the dog trot, he saw the rain sheeting down, along with an even stronger wind. He entered the front room of the south wing and tried to look like he wasn't in pain.

Roxanna half sat, half lay in a chair near the hearth. She sat up a bit when her uncle brought them coffee, and she held her cup in both hands trying to keep it steady. Ben's heart went out to her. He remembered how sick he'd felt the first time he killed a man. He took off his coat and hat and hung them up, then sat nearby as Hack slid onto his big chair.

"Honey, are you all right now?" Hack asked Roxanna.

She sipped the coffee and shuddered, then nodded.

"I know they weren't after you," Hack said, "but no more riding for a while."

She drew her hand across her eyes as if swiping tears away. "You don't have to worry. I never want that to happen, ever again."

"You did the right thing," Hack told her.

She drank more coffee. "You should have seen Ben's shot," she said, not looking at either of them. "From the saddle. And the gunman was so far away, high in the trees. And moving."

"That's why Ben's here." Hack cast him an admiring grin, then sobered. "So now both Kendalls are dead, and Sloan was right. It don't make no sense."

"Maybe it does," Roxanna said slowly, "if you think about it. Vera Kendall has everything now."

Hack frowned. "She's such a gentle woman. I can't see her as a killer."

"Men are such fools." Roxanna stared into her cup. "She's a witch."

Hack paid her no heed. "Frye could be the problem. Maybe he thinks he can take over Vera and the ranch."

They heard horses near the corrals as more of the men rode in, and Hack stood up and went outside under the dog trot to wait for a report.

Roxanna huddled in her chair. She wiped her eyes again, as if impatient at more tears.

Ben leaned forward. "You did what you had to do."

"I'm not as tough as I thought."

"You're tough enough."

She set her cup down and stood, staring into the crackling fire. Ben had the sense she'd have left the room, only she didn't want to be alone just now. Even if the only other person here was him.

He got up and went to her side. Slowly, he slid his right arm around her. She turned into his embrace, her face buried against his leather vest.

It had been more than three years since he'd held a woman in his arms. Holding Roxanna brought a flood of painful memories he'd long suppressed. His right hand rested on her lustrous hair. The tingling touch sizzled through him.

She felt soft and warm as she whispered, "I'm glad you're here, Ben."

She lifted her face and leaned back a little, gazing up at him in wonder. She had tears on her cheeks but had stopped shivering. Her lips were inches from his chin.

He held her a little tighter. She slid a hand up his chest.

Slowly, his heart drumming, Ben bent his head. She rose on her tiptoes. He could feel her warm breath on his face. He leaned closer, and his lips found the sweet velvet of hers. They kissed long and tenderly. She withdrew gently and pressed her face to his chest again. He wrapped both arms around her, ignoring the sting from his injury. He had not expected to feel charged with new life, just from having her in his arms.

He looked up, over Roxanna's head, and saw Hack in the doorway.

Stone-faced, the rancher closed the door behind him with a bang. Roxanna jumped, abruptly freed herself from Ben's embrace, and stumbled around until she fell into her chair. Hack looked grim, but Ben swore there was a twinkle in his eye. "What's going on here?"

Roxanna dabbed at her eyes. "I was falling apart, and Ben

held me, that's all."

"It weren't all."

"I thanked him for saving my life."

Her cheeks were rose pink, and Hack relented. "All right, honey. Why don't you go lie down awhile before supper?"

"I'll cook it," Ben said.

She smiled a little, avoiding Ben's gaze, then stood and left the room.

Ben sat near Hack, who frowned as he took his usual big chair. "I think a lot of that girl, Ben."

"I know, Mr. Larabee."

"Oh, so I catch you kissing her, and it's 'Mr. Larabee' again."

"I figured it better be."

Hack groaned and leaned back. "No, Ben, it's all right. This ain't been an easy day for any of us. And at least she stopped fighting you."

"Wait'll she tastes my cooking."

"*Can* you cook?"

"No, but I figure between the two of us, we can come up with something."

Hack snorted, then sobered. "With both Kendalls dead, no telling what will happen now or who it'll come from."

Ben nodded. "I figure Reilly will need help, no matter how many deputies he has."

"Yep. Something's sure going on."

Windows rattled, and they heard another sudden rush of heavy rain on the roof.

As evening fell, Vera Kendall stood in the parlor of the Lazy K ranch house and admired her reflection in the mirror on the back wall. Her blue satin dress set off her blonde hair just right, tied back in a matching ribbon. The lamps burned low, but the fire on the hearth crackled bright and hot in contrast to the storm outside.

The rain, heavy on the roof, brought wind that rattled the front windows. The noise almost masked the sound of the front door opening and closing. Frye came in, dropped his wet coat in the front room, and strode into the parlor. He removed his hat and kept it in hand.

Vera accepted his admiring look as her due, then moved to sit on the settee. He walked closer. "Where's Conchita?"

"Upstairs."

Frye sat next to her. "Miles is dead. Over on Larabee's place."

She looked at him curiously. "I thought you were going to wait."

"I guess our two men from Texas were in a hurry to get paid."

"So pay them."

Frye twirled his hat. He was trying not to look surprised, likely at her lack of shock. "They're both dead. The girl got one of them. Hawks shot the other out of the saddle."

Startled, she stared at him. "So Ben Hawks is still alive," she said. "And I have to be at Miles' funeral."

"Just wear your black veil. And remember what a great actress you are."

"I still worry."

"Don't, because Dejado's coming."

She hugged herself and leaned back against the cushions.

"Everything's going your way," he said. "But what's in it for me now that both Kendalls are dead?"

She smiled. "A lot of money."

"It's not what I had in mind."

She frowned at his faint smile. "Don't say that."

The smile faded. "There's two men in jail who might talk if they don't get off."

"Brian knows what he's doing."

"He's still a dandy, a real dude, and you know it. I was a better man for you, Vera."

"A lawyer with no money?"

"I'd just opened my office. It takes time to build a practice. You might have waited."

For a moment his annoyance gave her pause. She knew how to handle him, though. She knew how to handle everyone. Even Brian, carefully. She had no trouble wrapping Frye around her littlest finger. "Harry, when my family lost everything, I was destitute. I had to go on the stage to survive. I had nothing until Brian came along."

He was still scowling. "I'm a lot smarter than he is."

"You rode with him."

"Because of you."

"He believed in what he was doing."

"Maybe during the war, but how about after? We were still robbing and killing. For what?"

"You stayed with him," she said.

"I was in deep by then. From the beginning, Brian Avery wanted only one thing. Power."

"But he's made us rich, Harry. Both of us. Please, don't ruin it for me."

"So you believe everything he says, that the end justifies the means?"

She didn't answer. Hopefully he'd take the hint and leave.

"I would never have let you marry another man," he said. "Not when you already had a husband."

"But you said it, Harry. The end does justify the means."

He got to his feet. "Just one thing. Maybe I'm not a lawyer anymore, but I can tell you this. Bigamy is a crime. And getting your name on the deed by fraudulent means is just as bad. You're the one they'd send to prison, not Brian."

Her face felt hot. "Stop," she said, then made an effort to gentle her tone. "It's not like you to be so cruel."

"I despise him for what he's done to you."

"If he heard you talk like this . . ."

"The day hasn't come that I can't beat him to the draw."

Anxiety knifed through her. "Please don't say that."

"And I see you're still wearing my rose perfume."

"Yes." She cast her gaze downward, a practiced move. "I still remember the performance when you first gave it to me."

He shifted his feet. "No matter what happens, I'll always love you, Vera."

She smiled sweetly. He donned his hat, grabbed his coat from the front room, and went back out into the rain.

Vera sat staring into the fire. She had everything she'd always wanted now, but Harry Frye didn't give her any peace. Just the same, she knew what was best for her. She stroked her satin dress, enjoying its richness beneath her fingers.

Pounded by night rain and wind, the streets in Carmody were quiet. A few sheltered lamps burned in front of dark stores, and lamplight seeped through the windows at the jail. No one was out on a night like this, not if they could help it.

Inside the Wagon Wheel Saloon, opposite the jail and just west of the express office, a husky gunman named Brownie felt his liquor. With a hairy face and sweat-stained hat, he sat alone at a corner table, watching the dripping wet cowhands gathering at the bar. A scowl on his rough, square face, he sipped his whiskey and waited. No women worked in the saloon, but at least the piano was in fine tune. The short, balding piano player sang the ballad he played in a sorrowful voice. The song made Brownie frown and pour himself another whiskey.

The piano player launched into the chorus again. "He was born a Texas Ranger, with a six-gun in his hand / And fell in love with a maiden, who died on the desert sand / Ben Hawks began his long, long trail, and he rides the starry sky / He's lightning fast, so back away, or surely you will die."

The saloon doors opened, and Brownie glanced up. A short, ugly man with curly hair came inside and looked around. He was dripping wet, like a drowned rat. He spotted Brownie, came over and pulled up a chair, and helped himself to the whiskey bottle, frowning at the piano player. "Damned fellow seems to know all the verses about Ben Hawks. Makes me sick, you want the truth."

Brownie grabbed his whiskey bottle back. "What took you so long, Tinsley? Brian sent for us days ago."

Tinsley gulped whiskey and wiped his mouth. "Don't give me no trouble."

"Pinkley and Posher are in jail. We got to get 'em out or shut 'em up. Brian ain't picky as to which."

Tinsley grimaced. "We did a lot of riding with them boys."

"Just the same, if they talk to save their own skins, we'll all hang."

"You didn't rat down in Mesilla four years ago, and Brian got you out."

Brownie made a face. "I ain't Posher or Pinkley. They got no guts."

Tinsley glared at the piano player. "Can't somebody shut him up?" He turned back to Brownie with a sigh. "All right. Let's plan."

Brownie grinned. "I got ole Molly to help us out. She's a big drinker and always needs money. She lives in a shack by the stable . . ."

CHAPTER ELEVEN

The next morning, Saturday, the sun came out as clouds hovered over the hills. Ben rode into town with Buckley, who'd recovered enough to be full of wild stories he made up as they went along. When they got to Carmody, Buckley went to the general store on errands for Hack, while Ben walked to the marshal's office. Reilly, alone and sitting at his desk drinking coffee, looked glad to see him.

"Any trouble?" Ben asked.

"Nope, but I hear you had plenty. And got shot."

Ben helped himself to some coffee and pulled up a chair. "Just a graze."

"Too bad about Miles."

"How are the prisoners?"

"Real quiet. My deputies are getting bored. The circuit judge will be here Monday. We'll be setting up for trial in the Wagon Wheel Saloon."

Ben made a face. "Whoever's behind the killings may not wait for the trial. There's no guarantee those two will get off, and dead men can't say a word."

"Maybe. So far, no one's tried anything."

The door opened, and a tall lanky man in a long dark coat with a little string tie and small-brimmed hat came through it. The stranger had a long face and pale blue eyes. His left ear lobe was missing.

He closed the door quietly behind him, then faced Reilly.

"Marshal, I'm Wallace Loophole. Here for the defendants."

Some name, Ben thought as the lawman stood up to shake the fellow's hand. "I heard of you, Mr. Loophole. You come all the way up from Mesilla for this? Who's paying you?"

Loophole didn't miss a beat. "That's confidential, Marshal."

Reilly gestured toward Ben. "This here's Ben Hawks. Works for Larabee."

Eyebrows raised in recognition of the name, Loophole nodded a greeting, then turned to Reilly again. "I'd like to see my clients."

"All right. Soon as I check you for weapons."

Loophole sighed as Reilly lifted the lawyer's coattails and then made him take the coat off so the marshal could inspect him all the way to his fancy boots. "No guns or knives. Good. Now I need to see some identification."

Loophole's face darkened. "This is an insult."

"I said I'd heard of you. Got no notion what Wallace Loophole looks like. You could be him, or anybody." Reilly folded his arms across his chest. Ben sipped coffee to hide his smile.

Loophole huffed, then dug in an inside coat pocket and brought out a small, cream-colored square. "Here's my calling card. Satisfied?"

Reilly looked the card over, then handed it to Ben, who made a show of doing the same. Loophole drew breath as if to protest, but kept his mouth shut. "Seems okay," Ben said, handing the card back to Reilly, who handed it to the lawyer.

"Go on, then," Reilly said. "You got fifteen minutes."

When the lawyer had gone to the cells and closed the door behind him, Reilly sat back down with a scowl. "Something ain't right, Ben. You gonna be in town tonight?"

"Reckon I'd better be."

The front door opened, and Buckley leaned inside. "Marshal,

you'd better get out here."

Ben and the lawman went outside into the morning sunlight. A wagon was just pulling up in front of the jail. The driver was stocky and hard-faced, in his forties at a guess, with heavy dark eyebrows and a thick black mustache. To his left sat a blonde-haired woman all in black, including her hat and a veil that obscured her face. From what Ben could see of her, she looked young. Two cowhands with rifles reined up behind the wagon.

The lawman tipped his hat. "I'm right sorry about Miles, Mrs. Kendall." He nodded toward the driver. "Mr. Frye."

Frye looked grim. "Sorry doesn't count for much, Marshal. First Laird Kendall and now his brother. We know who's behind it. And maybe we know how to end it."

"Hold it right there," Reilly said. "I got two of your men locked up for trying to kill Roxanna Larabee and Buckley here. Ain't nothing going to happen in this valley unless I say so."

Frye glared at him, then shifted his harsh gaze to Ben. Reilly cleared his throat. "Mrs. Kendall, this youngster here is Buckley, and that's Ben Hawks."

She nodded, but didn't speak or lift her veil. Still in mourning, Ben figured.

Frye grunted. "I'll see Mrs. Kendall to the hotel, and then I'll take care of Miles." He circled the wagon and took her to the front of the hotel across the street. Ben watched him help her down and follow her inside, carrying her luggage.

Reilly grunted and pulled his hat back on. Buckley twirled his own hat in his hands. "I don't like the way things are going, Marshal. Frye is one mean hombre. Laird and Miles Kendall weren't too friendly, but at least they had good sense. Now they're both dead. Who's next?"

That night, Harry Frye joined Loophole in his hotel room. They sat with a bottle of whiskey by lamplight, and Loophole leaned back in his chair as they discussed Posher and Pinkley.

"The evidence is pretty strong," Loophole said. "Hawks has those boys dead to rights on what they did by the ridge at the Crooked Spur."

Frye grimaced. "We have to get them out. Pay them to disappear."

"That's not the way to handle this."

"What they say in court might hurt Vera Kendall. She's an innocent bystander."

"I'll make sure it's a fair trial."

"They have four witnesses," Frye said. "The Larabee girl and Buckley. And Ben Hawks. And Hack Larabee. How will you handle that?"

"Bias, my friend."

"I'm not your friend, and I don't trust lawyers. I know, because I was one."

Loophole made a face. "Well, that's rather amazing to hear. What happened to you?"

"The war."

Loophole nodded slowly. "You'll have to trust me, like it or not. I want your word you won't try to engineer any jailbreaks before the trial."

"I can't make any promises." Frye poured himself more whiskey. "Who shot off your earlobe?"

"A dissatisfied client."

"Well, if you don't succeed in this case, you'd better worry about more than a chunk of ear."

"Don't threaten me, Frye."

"No threat. Just a fact."

"The Kendall ranch, not you, is paying me. And that client who shot at me?" He smirked. "I'm still breathing. He's not."

A short while later, Frye slipped into Vera's room down the hall.

She was still fully dressed, dashing his hopes even before she snapped at him in a charged whisper. "You're taking a big chance coming here."

"No one saw me."

She fussed with her hair. "Why *are* you here, Harry?"

"We can't let Posher or Pinkley testify. Brian agrees."

Was it his imagination, or did she pale a little in the lamplight? "So what are you going to do?"

"It's Saturday night. It'll be noisy. Especially with that new piano at the Wagon Wheel."

She pursed her lips. "Be sure they get Ben Hawks at the same time."

"Don't worry. Haven't I always protected you?" He moved toward her. She backed away. He scowled. "Brian doesn't deserve you."

Vera stepped around him and reached for the doorknob. "I'm afraid of him, and you should be, too."

She opened the door, her meaning clear as day. As he stepped into the hall, she closed and locked the door behind him.

At the jailhouse, Reilly and Ben were on their fifth game of checkers. Ben kept winning. "Going to be a long night," Reilly said.

"So where are your deputies?"

"Jordan's at one end of town and Payson's at the other." Reilly smoothly jumped four of Ben's checkers and won the game. "You see, Ben, you got to keep your mind on what you're doing."

Ben leaned back in his chair and took up his coffee cup. The lamps burned low, and it felt cold despite the stove and shuttered windows. "What do you know about Harry Frye?"

"Nothing. I checked on him once. No one ever heard of him by that name before he turned up here. But he's a mean one."

"Wonder where he stands in this?"

"With the Lazy K ranch all to herself, the Widow Kendall won't be interested in no ramrod," Reilly said. "Maybe a fancy dude like Chandler Strong."

"She can inherit?"

"Laird Kendall put her name right on the deed with his and his brother's."

"Pretty trusting," Ben said.

"She twisted him around her little finger."

They set up another game, and Ben stoked the fire with some more wood. He could hear Pinkley and Posher snoring in the back cells. "They're pretty confident," he said. "No worries keeping 'em awake."

A woman's shrill scream pierced the night, from the alley just west of the jail.

"Could be a trick," Reilly said as he stood.

"You stay in here," Ben said. "I'll go."

Reilly shook his head. "This is my job. You bar the door."

"Maybe we'd better both have a look."

"No, Ben. You stay. They may try to get in here while I'm gone."

The woman screamed again. "Help! Somebody help me!"

Reilly turned the lamps down even further and unbarred the door. Ben stood nearby, six-gun in hand. Reilly took up a shotgun, jerked the door open, and flattened himself to one side of it. No shots came. Reilly waited a few more seconds, then ducked out. Ben pulled the door shut, but barely had time to heft the bar when a volley of rifle fire thudded into the outside wall.

Ben yanked the door open.

Reilly knelt on the sidewalk, hunched and bleeding. More rifle fire blasted away, bullets singing by Ben's head. One of them scorched his right cheek. He reached down, grabbed Reilly by the arm, and dragged him inside. Shouts and running footsteps from down the street told him the deputies were coming. He couldn't spare a thought for them right now. He kicked the door shut as another hail of bullets slammed into it.

Ben dropped to one knee and turned Reilly over. Blood glistened on the lawman's left arm, shoulder, and thigh. He looked up at Ben with round eyes, mouth open, unable to speak from the shock.

"Hang in there," Ben said. He slid his arms under Reilly's and dragged him over to the cot. With great effort, he lifted the groaning man and lowered him onto the blankets. Then he tore open Reilly's shirt, grabbed a bottle from the desk, and poured whiskey on the wounds.

Reilly started to cuss as Ben felt around for lead. "What the devil are you doing, trying to kill me?"

Relief overcame Ben. "Bullets went clean through, but you need a doctor."

"Never mind," Reilly grunted. "We may be dead by morning."

Across the street, Brownie and Tinsley drew out of sight into the alley.

"I hit 'im good," Brownie said.

"Yeah, but now what? Pinkley and Posher are still in there. And Hawks ain't even hurt."

Brownie made a face. "We need another plan." He led the way back through the alley.

CHAPTER TWELVE

Someone pounded at the jailhouse door. "Marshal? Ben? It's Buckley. There's two guys shot dead in the street out here, got deputy badges on. You all right?"

Ben rose from Reilly's side. The kid was going to get himself killed. "Get away from there. And get the doc. Then head out to the Crooked Spur, tell Hack what happened."

"Be morning afore I get back."

"Just get going."

He went back to the cot where Reilly lay and did his best to keep the lawman comfortable. A short time later, a knock at the door and a few murmured words heralded the doctor's presence. Ben let him in and barred the door behind him. The young medic adjusted his spectacles and removed his coat.

"You took a chance," Reilly moaned.

"Nobody ever shoots a doctor," the medic said. "Especially the only one for fifty miles around. Now you lie still."

A yell came from the cells in the back. "What's going on out there?"

Ben went through the rear door and turned up the lamp that hung opposite the cells. Pinkley was in one of them, Posher in the other. Ben nodded toward the tiny barred windows high up in each cell's rear wall. "If I were you, I'd stay under those windows and not in front of 'em."

Pinkley paused at the bars, then hurried back to the wall, glaring up at the window above his head. Posher stood back, his mouth working. He rubbed his flat nose. "Maybe someone wants us out."

"Maybe someone wants you dead."

"Turn that lamp back down," Pinkley muttered.

Ben lowered the wall lamp to a soft glow, then returned to the marshal's office, closing the rear door behind him. He'd made his point. The two hired guns would be too scared to move now, let alone cause any trouble.

In the noisy saloon, Tinsley and Brownie huddled at a corner table, drinking whiskey and playing cards. Tinsley whispered, "You think Reilly's dead?"

Brownie shook his head. "I don't know. He's a tough old bird."

"We shot him full of holes, and the deputies are dead, so that means Hawks is all by his lonesome. But we got to be sure."

A new voice broke in. "Sure of what?" Frye sauntered up to the table, plunked a drink down, and pulled out a chair. "Don't tell me you boys didn't get the job done with all that ruckus."

Brownie scowled. "Judge don't get here till Monday, so we got tomorrow night. But we got to get someone inside that jail, find out about the marshal."

Tinsley shook his head. "Even if Reilly's alive, he ain't in no shape to shoot back."

Frye gulped his whiskey, snagged their bottle, and poured himself another. "You boys have got some explaining to do. Who wants to start?"

Ben sat by Reilly, who lay on his cot, his left arm in a sling. Heavily bandaged, Reilly cussed under his breath.

"Your ma would tan your hide," Ben said, sipping coffee, "if she heard how you was talking."

"My ma's in Philadelphia with her cats. Where's yours?"

"In Texas, where she belongs."

Reilly opened his eyes. "Where she belongs? That's how you talk about your ma?"

"If you ever met her, you'd send her back. She's a holy terror."

Reilly tried to grin, then winced in pain. "What time is it?"

Ben pulled out his watch. "Nearly four."

"I'm sorry you sent for Hack. They may be laying for 'im."

"Hack's no fool," Ben said. "They didn't make him a major for nothing. Besides, you're in bad shape."

"Not so bad. The doc said the bullets didn't do any real damage. Just lost a lot of blood. I'll be up and around afore you know it."

Reilly slept after that, and Ben paced up and down, trying to stay awake. The jail was like a small fortress, but there were desperate men out there. A sharp rap at the door cut through his fatigue. "Marshal Reilly? Open up."

The voice was familiar, though Ben couldn't place it. He went to the door and called through it. "Who's there? What do you want?"

"Name's Frye. Who're you? I know you ain't the marshal. Let me in. I want to see Reilly."

Ben glanced back at the dozing marshal. Whatever Frye wanted, it couldn't be good, especially at this hour. "He's asleep. Come back after sunrise." He returned to his chair by the cot, ignoring Frye's repeated knocking until the man gave up and left. Only after several minutes of silence had passed did Ben let himself relax.

Finally, near dawn, he dozed off.

More pounding on the jailhouse door. Ben opened bleary eyes and saw Sunday morning sunlight peeking around the edges of the window shutters. What now? He hauled himself upright and headed toward the noise. "Who's there?"

"It's Hack, son. Open up."

Relief shot through Ben. He unbarred the door and opened it. Hack Larabee stood there, with Roxanna and Sloan. Beyond them were four more ranch hands from the Crooked Spur. "You and the hands stay out here but close," Hack said to Sloan. Then he and Roxanna entered the jailhouse.

Ben frowned at Roxanna as she stepped over the threshold. "You got no business here."

She drew herself up, balancing her Winchester. "I can out-shoot you any day, Ben Hawks."

Hack threw her a stern look. "You get on over to the hotel and get us a couple of rooms. Have Sloan go with you."

Roxanna's face flushed rosy red. "You men think you're the only ones can do anything around here. Well, I'm not going."

"I'm your uncle, and I say you're going."

"You're my partner, and I got a fifty-fifty say in this. I'm not leaving, Uncle Henry."

Hack loomed over her. "Young woman, you do as I say."

She tried to stand taller. "No."

Ben stepped forward and faced Roxanna, glaring down into her eyes. Her hair lay in waves on her shoulders, its color and shine setting off her lovely face and pouting lips, but he refused to be distracted. "You get over to the hotel. Right now."

"You can't tell me what to do."

"Well, I'm telling you."

"I'm not moving. And you can't make me."

Ben wasn't sure how it happened, but suddenly his hands were at her waist and he was drawing her up against him. He bent his head and kissed her hard. She sagged in his hold, her hat falling back from its chin strap.

When he released her, she fell back a few steps, out of breath, the Winchester lifted in her hands. Her cheeks burned like fire, her dark eyes glazed. She hesitated, then turned and walked slowly to the door. Her hand on the latch, she spoke without turning. "I'll get the rooms, Uncle Hack."

Hack stared as she went out the door. He closed it and set the bar across it. He turned to glare at Ben, who swallowed hard, sweat damp on his brow. "You got a lot of nerve, Ben Hawks. And it's Mr. Larabee to you from now on."

Ben, still shaken, had no idea why he had kissed Roxanna again, but it sure felt pretty good. Maybe he hadn't died three years ago, after all.

Reilly turned his head. "Maybe it don't matter none, but I'm the one who got shot around here. You bring any more men with you, Hack?"

"Sloan and a bunch of the boys, but only Sloan's any good with a gun. The others, they can shoot snakes. That's about it."

"We got our share of snakes," Reilly said.

Still dazed from Ben's kiss, Roxanna crossed the street under a clear sky. Sloan escorted her to the hotel entrance, then walked toward the Wagon Wheel. She took a moment to collect herself, then went in.

As she entered the lobby, she saw Frye coming down the stairs. He looked her over, tipped his hat, and continued on outside. She followed him to the hotel doorway and stood there, watching him head for the Wagon Wheel, gripping her Winchester tight. A silky voice caught her attention. "Miss Roxanna, you look radiant."

She glanced toward the speaker. Chandler Strong paused in front of her, bowing slightly, hat in hand. He followed her as she backed into the lobby. "Hello, Chandler."

"Are you here for breakfast? Care to join me?"

"I rode half the night to get here. I'm taking a room so I can get some sleep."

He smiled. "Even so, you look lovely."

"I guess you heard about Miles Kendall."

"Yes, it was very sad."

"And the attempted jailbreak last night?"

"My, yes, I heard about that. But that has nothing to do with us." He reached out and took her hand. "Though we live in dangerous times, Miss Roxanna. Times when a young woman like you needs a good man to protect her." He drew her hand to his lips and bowed again.

She slid it from his grasp, wishing she dared wipe it on her skirt. "And you've been a good friend. But I must get some sleep." Before he could say anything more, she turned and went to the front desk, where she awakened the elderly clerk and arranged for two rooms, one for herself and one for her uncle. Then she went up the stairs, so weary she could hardly climb them.

She had barely reached the landing when she saw Vera Kendall, fully dressed, coming out of the water closet. Vera looked startled, then gave her a cool nod. "Miss Larabee. I didn't expect to see you here."

Two awkward encounters in as many minutes. "I'm sorry about Miles," Roxanna said, while part of her thought, *shouldn't Vera be saying that to me?*

Vera glanced downward. "Yes, and now I'm all alone. Mr. Frye tries to help, but it's not the same. If only Laird were still alive."

"I know Laird was very much in love with you."

Vera smiled, her blue eyes misty. "Yes, he was."

Some devil must have prompted what Roxanna said next. "What do you know about how he died?"

Vera glared at her. "By the size of that rifle you're holding, I should be asking you that question. Good day, Miss Larabee." She spun on her heel and continued down the hall to her room.

Roxanna made a face at Vera's retreating back. Then she went to her own room, slamming the door shut behind her. She stalked to the window and looked down. To her left, far along the boardwalk, she saw Chandler Strong entering the Wagon Wheel Saloon. Closer to the hotel, Buckley was parked on the bench outside the express office. Only a few others were stirring. Over at the jail, the door remained closed tight.

The rattle of wheels drew her attention in the opposite direction. Coming up the street in the early morning sun was the stage from Mesilla, the high vehicle rocking on its leather hinges and throwing its passengers around.

Wearily, she turned toward her bed.

Inside the jailhouse, Ben dozed on a chair while the doctor checked on Reilly and coffee steamed on the iron stove. Hack, standing nearby, watched as the doctor closed his bag and spoke to Reilly, who sat propped against some pillows on his cot. "Marshal, you'll be all right, but you stay put."

After the doctor left, Hack handed Reilly a cup of coffee and a chunk of cinnamon bread, then pulled up a chair. "You listen to what that young man said. Those two prisoners ain't worth dying for."

"Ben Hawks thinks they are."

Hack looked over at Ben. "Yeah, well, he was a Texas Ranger. They don't have no sense."

Reilly tried to grin. "So what are you doing here?"

A pounding at the door cut off Hack's reply. He froze. The pounding got louder.

Ben jerked awake. A woman's sharp voice carried over the pounding. "Marshal, open this door!"

For the first time since Hack met him, Ben looked nervous. "Now we're in for it," he said. "That's my mother."

Chapter Thirteen

Hack stood up, and Reilly stared at Ben. "Your ma?" the lawman asked.

Ben nodded. "Ever since my father died twenty years ago, she's been a real terror."

"Why is she here?" Hack demanded.

"She knows I'm after Avery," Ben said. "And now we're in for it."

"She's just a woman," Hack countered. "What are you afraid of?" Not waiting for an answer, the rancher walked over and unbarred the door.

Ben's mother charged inside, shoving Hack out of the way. A petite, fiery woman in her early fifties, her black hair shoulder-length and streaked with a little gray, she wore a simple traveling dress with a cape. Both garments were dusty from the road. Her mouth was set in a hard frown, and above her high cheekbones, her large brown eyes flashed in anger. "Where's my son? Oh, there you are, you bad boy."

Ben was the first to recover. He was somewhat used to the surge of energy his mother brought with her wherever she went. He removed his hat, took a step forward and kissed her cheek, then backed away. She glared at him, then at Hack, who wore a look of shock as he turned from barring the door, and finally at the wounded lawman, who sat on his cot staring at her in disbelief.

Ben cleared his throat. "Ma, this is Marshal Reilly and Hack Larabee."

"The outlaw?" Eyebrows raised, she looked Hack over until he reddened. Then she gazed around the jail. "What's going on here?"

"Attempted jail break," Hack said crisply, as if a firm tone could retrieve his dignity.

"I didn't ask you. I asked the marshal."

Hack tried again. "Look, ma'am, this ain't no place for you."

"I'm no 'ma'am' to you," she snapped. "I'm Sara Hawks, and Ben wrote he came up here because the marshal had information on his fiancée's murder. If Avery's gang is in these parts, Ben could be killed. I want to know what's going on, right now."

Ben shrugged. "The marshal found the stage driver's watch on a dead cowhand."

She listened in silence and helped herself to a sip of Hack's coffee as Ben told her what he had learned. When he finished, she set Hack's cup down.

"I just spent two days on a rocking box made by the Devil himself," she said, her voice lower but still brisk. "I had to hang my head out the window to avoid some man's smelly cigar. I slept with one eye open. I'm stiff and sore and black and blue, and I'm angry and real hungry. And this coffee tastes like soot. Ben, you have to take me to breakfast."

"I can't leave here," Ben said.

Reilly grunted. "Take your ma to breakfast. Hack will stay with me."

Sara Hawks looked Hack over again, skeptically, then turned to Ben. "One of the men on the stage was a judge."

"We've been waiting for him."

"And another was a killer."

Ben frowned. "What makes you think that?"

"Everyone was afraid of him. They called him Dejado."

Ben felt suddenly cold. He looked at Reilly, who sat stone-faced on the edge of his cot, and Hack, who grimaced. "That's all we need," Reilly muttered.

"Well, we know why he's here," Hack said. "He's after Ben."

Sara made a face. "Ben, take me to breakfast. Once I've got some food in me, and had a nap, we can plan." She traced a line in the dust on the desk and eyed Reilly as Ben pulled on his hat. "Don't you ever clean this place up?" Then she shot another feisty look at Hack Larabee. The rancher seemed at a loss for words, though Ben wasn't surprised. His mother affected a lot of folks that way.

Feeling like he was marching to his own funeral, Ben reluctantly went out the door with her, leaving the other two men to stare after them.

The hotel had a small restaurant inside, just beyond the lobby. Only one other patron, a plump merchant type in a Sunday-best suit, had been seated, and he was getting up to leave as they walked in. Apart from the old man who was serving them, Ben and Sara had the place to themselves.

While they ate their breakfast, Sara Hawks listened as Ben told her everything. She shook her head as he finished and raised her coffee cup. "You have to realize, Ben, you may never find Avery. All you've been doing for three years is getting into all kinds of trouble. I lost your father, and I'm terrified I'm going to lose you. And if Avery is in these parts, he knows why you're here. You'll be shot in the back, ambushed. And for what? You can't change what happened to Lora."

Ben gazed into his cup, watching the steam rise. "She used to walk in my dreams, but now I can't even see her face."

She hesitated. "I still have the locket. Would you like it back?"

"Not until this is over."

117

She laid a hand on his wrist. "Growing up, all you wanted to be was a lawman, like your father. I think you had it in your mind to find whoever shot him down, but you never could, because no one knew who it was. Now you're in the same frame of mind. What about your own life, son?"

"Avery's here. I can smell it."

Sara drew back, lips pursed, and mercifully let it go.

After breakfast, they went to the desk to get her a room, but the elderly hotel clerk shook his head. "Miss Larabee took the last two rooms. One for her and one for her uncle, Hack Larabee."

"That man at the jail?" Sara snapped. "I'll take his room."

"You can have mine," Ben said.

"No, I'll take Hack Larabee's."

"Why?"

"Never you mind. It's the room I want."

The clerk wrinkled his nose. "Ma'am, I'm sorry, but you can't just—"

"Mr. Larabee can bunk with me," Ben said.

The clerk gave him a wide-eyed look, then shrugged. "Hack's gonna be mad, but all right. If you say so."

Sara glanced at Ben. "My luggage is at the express office. I'd thank you to go get it."

Ben nodded and turned to the clerk. "Anyone else from the stage take a room?"

"Yeah, a judge and a salesman. And another fellow, a real mean customer who just made his mark when he signed in."

After fetching the luggage and seeing his mother settled, Ben returned to the jail. Reilly lay sleeping, and Hack was making fresh coffee. The morning, still overcast, seemed peaceful at the moment.

"You know, Ben," Hack said, "if you want to quit working for me, I'll understand."

"I ain't leaving."

"Dejado wants to be the man who got Ben Hawks. And I figure he'll make it a fair fight for show. But why get yourself killed? Think of your mother."

"Leave her out of this."

Hack smiled. "She's some woman."

"What do you mean by that?"

"She's a right handsome female, Ben."

"Mr. Hawks to you," Ben snapped.

Hack grinned, then yawned. "Coffee's done. Might as well go over to the hotel. I could use some shut-eye."

"You don't have a room."

Hack frowned. "What?"

"The hotel was full up, so my mother took yours away from you."

Hack gaped at him. Then, just for a moment, happiness lit his face.

"Forget it," Ben ordered. "You can bunk with me."

Things stayed quiet all day, though Ben didn't trust the calm. He, Reilly, and Hack all knew the danger wasn't past. When evening fell, Ben and Hack opened cans of beans for supper. Reilly ate sitting up against a pillow while Ben held his plate.

"Trial's in the morning," Reilly said, scooping up a forkful of beans with his good arm. "And the judge is settled in at the hotel, safe and sound."

Hack grunted. "Can't happen soon enough. I won't rest easy 'til everything's over."

Soberly, Ben eyed Hack. After almost a week in the rancher's company, he was pretty near certain Hack wasn't Brian Avery—

just a man caught up in a range war he didn't want but couldn't stop. "None of us will."

As soon as she'd woken from her long afternoon nap, Roxanna had ordered a hot bath. Now she headed down the lamplit upstairs hallway toward the small bathing room, wearing her blue dressing gown, a big towel over her arm, auburn hair pinned up high on her head.

When she opened the bathing-room door, she was startled to see a woman she didn't know, settling deep in the big iron tub filled with hot water and bubbles. Roxanna stormed inside, slamming the door behind her. "That's my water!"

The woman in the tub turned around and glared at her. In the wavering glow from the lamp on a nearby table, Roxanna saw she was older, with some gray in her black hair and fine lines in her handsome face. "How dare you come in here?" the woman snapped. "Didn't you see the sign on the door? Besides, I got here first."

Roxanna walked over to the tub and glared down at the interloper, hands on her hips. "You're a rude woman."

"I just spent forty-eight hours on the stagecoach. What have you been doing, needlepoint?"

Furious, Roxanna laid a hand on the woman's head and shoved her under. The woman's knees rose sharply, water splashing all over. Roxanna let go and the woman came up sputtering, her hair wet. She dabbed at her tight-shut eyes.

"I'm Roxanna Larabee, and I happen to be in the saddle ten hours a day. I work just as hard as my Uncle Hack, and a lot harder than some fancy woman who has time to gallivant around the country."

The older woman wiped her eyes one last time, then glared up at Roxanna. "Your uncle's that man at the jail?"

Thrown by the question, Roxanna hesitated. How did this

person know Uncle Hack? "He's over there, yes."

"With that wild Ben Hawks?"

Roxanna drew herself up. "He's not wild."

The woman's gaze sharpened. "You know Ben Hawks?"

"Everyone knows him."

"Well, so do I. I'm Sara Hawks. He's my son."

Supper was long since finished. Reilly had dropped off again, and Ben and Hack sat drinking coffee to keep awake. "So," Hack said after a while, his gaze on the potbellied stove in the corner. "What brought you out here to Carmody? Like I said when I hired you on, you're too good a gunslinger to settle for a hundred a month. You ready to tell me the real story?"

Ben thought it over, and decided he was. He found it easier to start than he'd expected, maybe because it was late and the night outside was so silent and still. "The woman I meant to marry died three years ago in a stage holdup east of Tucson. She and five others. We know it was Brian Avery's gang."

"I heard about it."

"I'm still hoping to track him down. I got word he could be in this part of the territory."

"You know what Avery looks like?"

"No. But your man Rossiter knew, and now he's dead."

Hack looked toward a shuttered front window as if he could see out of it. "Why do you think Rossiter was with Avery?"

"Marshal said he was."

"Rossiter kept to himself. We figured it was the Lazy K shot him down."

"Maybe so. Or maybe not."

After a long pause, Hack spoke without meeting Ben's eyes. "There's something you need to know, Ben. If you've been at this for three years, you're wasting your life. I know from experience. Hate takes a lot out of a man. Drains all the life out of you. At some point, you have to give it up. Before it's too late to change."

"Not easy."

Hack finally glanced at him. "Wasn't for me either. But Roxanna dragged me out of it."

"I have to admit," Ben said, "I've started having conversations with myself."

"I did the same."

"But it would be a rotten thing if Avery got away with it."

Hack leaned forward, cradling his coffee cup. "Now we've known each other a time, I figure it's not a need for vengeance driving you, which don't set well with the Lord. I can see it's justice you want, and that's something to admire. But you ought to think about getting your life back. Why let Avery have it?"

"Maybe you're right, but I'm pretty sure Avery's somewhere around this valley."

Hack took a long moment to answer, then shook his head. "I wish you luck, Ben. And I hope you live long enough to tell the story to your grandkids."

Back in the hotel wash room, Roxanna stared at Sara Hawks in dismay. "Ben is your son?"

"Yes. Want to fight about it?"

Roxanna gaped a moment more, then burst out laughing. She turned to sit on a nearby chair, her face rosy as she tried to stop her mirth. "I'm sorry. I mean, Ben works for us."

"So he said. He's only there to find the men who killed his sweetheart."

Ben had never mentioned that, at least not to her. Flustered, Roxanna played with her towel. "I'm sorry."

Sara let out a sigh, and went on almost as if she'd forgotten she was talking to a total stranger. "But it's been three years, and he's driving himself into a frenzy over it. He won't look at another woman because Lora was the only woman who ever got to him. And now he's wasting his life."

Roxanna took that in, then drew a deep breath and spoke. "He kissed me."

"What?"

"Twice."

Now it was Sara Hawks' turn to stare. After a long moment, she reached for her towel. "Lora was a perfect angel, or so Ben thought, and you certainly are not. What's the attraction?"

"Maybe it's that I don't put up with strangers being rude to me," Roxanna snapped.

Sara held her gaze, as if trying to stare her down. After a long moment, one corner of Sara's mouth twitched. "Turn your back."

Roxanna turned away. She heard water lapping and splashing as Sara came up out of the tub. The woman ducked behind the screen and came out shortly after, wearing a dressing gown and rubbing a towel over her wet hair. "My son actually kissed you?"

Embarrassed and defensive, Roxanna nodded.

Sara frowned. "Seems I'm here just in time to straighten things out."

Something thumped and then scraped against the back wall of Pinkley's cell. The big gunslinger snorted as he woke from a half-doze. "Wha . . . ? What was that?"

In the cell next door, Posher caught his eye. "Maybe Brian's gonna bust us out," he said, hopefully.

"Or kill us." Pinkley bit his lip. It was hard to see with the lamp low, but he cocked his head and eyed the small window high in the cell wall. Something clinked against the bars, then clinked again. A muffled curse followed.

Pinkley and Posher watched in nervous silence. Then Posher gestured upward with his cuffed hands. "Look!"

Pinkley gaped in surprise. Through the window in each cell, a revolver jerked between the bars and dangled on a length of rawhide thong. Whoever was on the other end slowly lowered the weapons within the gunslingers' reach.

Grinning, Posher grabbed for his. Too late, he saw the thong was caught on the hammer, holding it back and ready to fire. As he tried to free it, the tangled six-gun went off with a roar. The shot thudded into the adobe floor. Startled, the big man jumped back. In the other cell, Pinkley fought to untangle the last knot from the second six-gun.

The door from the marshal's office burst open.

Ben Hawks came charging in with his Colt in hand. Posher froze. Pinkley twisted the still-bound weapon he held, trying to move it around to fire. Ben was faster, and pulled the trigger. His bullet hit Pinkley's left boot, barely missing his big toe. Pinkley jumped, then froze, horrified, as Ben snapped at them. "All right, get away from those six-shooters."

Hack Larabee came hurrying in with a shotgun. Both prisoners threw their hands up.

"Get down on the floor," Ben ordered. "Face down. Flat."

Pinkley swore under his breath, but he and Posher did as ordered. While Hack held the shotgun, Ben entered the cells and retrieved the weapons, using a knife to slice the rawhide thongs. "Keep an eye on our friends here while I bring these out to Reilly. Then we'll figure out what to do with these damn fools."

"Shoulda told a couple of my hands to guard the alley," Hack muttered. "Whoever tried to sneak those guns in is gone by now." He held his shotgun steady while Ben ducked into the office with the six-guns and returned a minute later empty-handed.

"We'll cuff 'em behind their backs," he said. "They can't do a blamed thing that way, and I'd as soon keep 'em locked up here as move 'em out front."

Pinkley opened his mouth to protest, then shut it at the rancher's steely glare. After cuffing both men, Ben and Hack locked the cells, turned the lamp down near to nothing, and departed, closing the door behind them.

Posher got up and stumbled around in the near darkness. "Whoever tried to help us, they don't know what they're doing."

"Well, they're gone now."

Posher sighed. "It's gonna be a long night."

Some time later, around midnight, Posher sat up in the near darkness, listening. His hands ached, and he hadn't slept much. A scuffling noise came from the alley outside the jail, then something thunked against the wooden wall.

"Psst," Posher hissed at Pinkley. "You hear that? They're coming for us. Brian's getting us out."

Pinkley blinked and struggled to sit up, one ear cocked. "I hear it." He chewed his lip. "You sure it's them again? The six-guns didn't work. We're getting out of here alive, ain't we?"

Posher squinted upward. "Can't see a blamed thing."

"What d'you think they're doing?"

"Keep your voice down," Posher hissed. "Don't want Hawks or Larabee coming in here." He strained at the cuffs around his wrists. "Try to get your hands free. We'll need to be able to ride."

Both men fell silent. Then, suddenly, he yelped. "Holy cow!"

Something dropped through the little barred window above Pinkley, spitting fire and smoke. A thick cylinder with a short fuse. It hit the floor and rolled into a corner. A second cylinder followed, this time through Posher's window.

"Help!" Pinkley shrieked. "Dynamite!"

The yell from the jail cells jolted Ben from his doze. He charged into the back room and skidded to a halt, Hack a step behind him. One look at the spitting sticks of dynamite, and Ben sprinted back into the office. He returned at a dead run with the keys and unlocked Posher's cell, then moved to Pinkley's.

"It's gonna blow!" Posher yelped.

Hack grabbed Posher and shoved him toward the front office, while Ben fought with the lock on Pinkley's cell. Pinkley looked ready to faint. The rancher hovered in the office doorway, until Ben shouted, "Get out of here, Hack!"

The cell lock clicked open, Ben grabbed Pinkley and shoved him toward safety. The big gunman crashed against the side of the office doorway and nearly fell. Ben pushed him on through.

The dynamite exploded in a deafening roar.

Ben sailed like a twig through the open doorway and into the office. The outside walls of the cell area collapsed inward. Iron bars clattered on the floor, and the back roof caved in with a thunderous rumble. The wall between the cells and front office wavered from the shock, and the door leaned on one hinge. Debris and dust clouded the room.

Ben crashed against the side of the stove and slid hard against the front wall. He lay dazed, crumpled up in a ball. The roar of the explosion had deafened him. He saw Hack kneeling next to him, speaking frantically, and Reilly up on his elbow on the cot, shouting at him, but he couldn't hear a word.

Behind Hack, a tongue of fire licked at the battered rear door frame. Ben tried to speak, point, anything, but had no strength to move. Hack glanced around, spotted the flames, and ran to stamp them out. Abruptly, he looked up toward the front door. Pinkley and Posher lay near it, pale and stunned-looking, lips moving like they were cussing. Hack paid them no mind as he hurried over. *Someone must be knocking,* Ben thought. Thinking took effort. His whole body hurt, especially his head. A little bit of hearing came back to him, and the muffled pounding registered. Then Buckley's voice, as if from down a well. "Marshal! Mister Larabee! Ben! Are you all right?"

Opening the door a crack, Hack peered outside into the dark. "Where's Sloan and the others?"

"Sloan and Mackay are coming. They were on watch at both ends of town. The others're sleeping, I guess."

"Get the doc. And keep them women out of here."

"What women?"

"You'll see." Hack closed the door and set the bar, then hurried back to Ben. "Come on. Let's get you off the floor."

Reilly spoke sharply. "Don't move 'im, Hack. His neck could be broken."

CHAPTER FOURTEEN

A roar louder than thunder jolted Roxanna from sound sleep. *What on earth . . . ?* Groggily, she sat up and reached for her dressing gown.

Her bedroom door burst open. Sara Hawks strode in, grabbed Roxanna's coat from the hook behind the door, and tossed it at her. "Someone blew up the jailhouse. Come on. We need to find out what happened."

They reached the jailhouse, or at least the part still standing, just as the doctor arrived at a run in his shirt sleeves. Hack let the doctor inside but then closed the door to a slit. Relief at the sight of her uncle apparently unharmed made Roxanna want to cry, even as she felt furious that Hack wouldn't let them in. Buckley, already a nervous wreck, backed away on the boardwalk as Sara Hawks pounded on the door.

"My son's in there," she shouted. "Let me see him. Ben!"

Hack opened up another inch, just enough to peer out at them. "Madam, get back to the hotel."

"I'm not your madam. Get out of my way."

"They tried to dynamite the prisoners. We could be next. Now get out of here."

Chin up, Sara fumed. "I want to know how my son is."

"Buckley, get them back to the hotel," Hack said, "and you park yourself in the lobby and keep 'em there." He shoved the door shut, and Roxanna heard the thump of the bar being set.

Sara stared at the closed door, then turned away. In the moonlight, her expression was bleak. Roxanna put her arm around her and realized Sara was trembling.

Buckley came over to them. "Best do as Hack says. We could all get shot out here."

Sara planted her feet, and Roxanna followed suit. "We're not moving," Sara said. "Not until I see Ben."

"Ma'am, Miss Roxanna, please!" Buckley's voice cracked. "Hack'll have my hide if I don't get you back where it's safe."

Roxanna didn't want to leave either, but she took pity on the young ranch hand. "All right. We'll go to the hotel, at least for long enough to get dressed."

Across the street in the Wagon Wheel, the piano had gone silent in the lamplight. At a center table, a drunk lay asleep with his head down. Cards and chips were scattered on other tables, and the barkeep snored sitting up behind the walnut bar. The only people awake in the near-empty saloon were an exhausted Brownie and Tinsley.

Frye strode in and joined them. He looked furious. "You lunkheads. Can't you do anything right?"

"Yell all you want," Brownie said, "but we got a trial coming up tomorrow. So what are you gonna do about it?"

"You have more dynamite?"

"No," Tinsley said. "That's all there was around here. This ain't no mining town."

"And I ain't rushing no jail," Brownie said.

Tinsley gulped his whiskey. "Maybe Loophole can get 'em off."

Frye shook his head. "If he doesn't, they may talk to keep from hanging."

Brownie gaped. "They're gonna hang when they didn't kill nobody?"

"This fellow's a hanging judge," Frye said. "And those boys know Brian's rules."

"Get off, get out, shut up, or die," Brownie grunted.

Frye grimaced. "The trial's going to be here, so the marshal or whoever has to get them across the street in the morning. You spread out and take cover, and make sure you get both of them while they're in the open. I've got others to back you up."

"We'll be spotted," Brownie complained. "How're we gonna get away?"

"Be smart about it," Frye snapped. "Just make sure you get Ben Hawks."

When first light hit the street on Monday, Ben lay asleep on a cot salvaged from the collapsed cell area and set near the dozing Reilly. The doctor had come and gone. Ben was lucky, he'd said—no serious injuries, just cuts and abrasions from splintered wood and a mild concussion from his hard landing. Hack thanked God for it.

The two prisoners snored quietly on blankets in the corner of the office, still with their hands cuffed behind them. Hack sat against the front wall with his rifle on his lap, trying to stay awake.

Posher stirred, then opened his eyes. "My head hurts. And my arms. You could've untied us at least."

Hack glared at him. "Are you ready to talk now?"

"Are you kidding?" Posher grumbled. "Only way we're gonna stay alive is if we keep our mouths shut."

"Didn't help you with the dynamite."

"No," Posher said, "but if we get off, they won't do nothing."

Someone knocked at the door. Hack struggled to his feet, rubbing his eyes. "Yeah?"

A sharp female voice answered. "It's Sara Hawks. Open up."

Hack slid the bar aside and opened the door, letting in the

morning sun. Standing with Sara was Roxanna, both fully dressed and holding trays of hot food. Buckley stood behind them with a larger tray.

"Well," Hack said, "now you're talking."

The women and Buckley came inside. Sara set her tray down on the table near Reilly's cot and hurried to her son's side. Roxanna followed suit, which didn't surprise Hack at all.

Sara shook Ben gently. He opened his eyes and smiled at her.

"I'm hungry," he said.

Sara helped Ben to his feet. Reilly awoke, and came to the table with Hack's assistance. They sat around the table, sharing the hot food. Hack cuffed the sleepy prisoners' hands in front of them, and Buckley fed them where they sat in the corner. While everyone ate, Sara kept glancing at her son.

Abruptly, another knock at the door came. "Like a blasted train station," Hack said, and went to answer it. He grunted as he stepped back and allowed the new arrival to enter. Wallace Loophole surveyed the crowded, dusty office with its heaps of half cleared debris and crooked back door.

"Well, Marshal," Loophole said, "you sure have a mess here."

Reilly frowned. "Don't give me no trouble, Loophole. Where were you last night?"

"In my room. Oh, I heard the noise, but it didn't keep me awake."

"Hey, lawyer," Pinkley said, chewing on some bacon. "We got to talk to you."

"They've already cleared the saloon for trial," Loophole said, "and they've picked a jury. The judge gave us half an hour. So if you don't mind, Marshal, I'd like to use your office to speak with my clients."

"No," Reilly said. "You can use the storeroom at the saloon."

"We ain't never gonna get across that street alive," Posher said.

Ben downed his coffee. "We'll give you cover."

"Yeah?" Pinkley grunted. "How you gonna do that?"

Loophole folded his arms and frowned. "Yes, Mr. Hawks. How are you going to get them across a wide-open street with rooftops and alleys where gunmen can lie in wait?"

"Don't worry about it," Ben said.

Hack stood. "You women get across with the lawyer here. We'll follow."

Sara stood up and faced him. Chest high to Hack, she glared up at him, her dark eyes flashing. "Will you stop telling us what to do?"

All that fire in such a small package. Hack wanted to laugh, but made himself look stern. "Listen to me, little woman, I'm the big he-bull in these parts."

"I'm not your little woman, and I'm no cow. I'm Ben Hawks' mother, and I'm staying."

Hack gripped her chin gently, tipping her head back. "Listen, little lady. If you and my niece ain't out of here in five seconds, I'm carrying you out."

"You and what army?"

"I'm all the army I need."

She was ready to keep fighting, Hack could tell, but Reilly forestalled her by getting to his feet. "We got a job to do," Reilly said. "And you women are in the way."

Roxanna took Sara's arm, pulling her away from Hack. "Come along, Sara. They're thickheaded. No use arguing with them."

Hack would've sworn both women hid smiles as they left.

When the women and Loophole were gone, Ben and Hack, with Buckley's help, got the prisoners through the ruined cell area and out behind the jail where horses were saddled and waiting. Several of Hack's men were there, including Sloan.

Reilly stayed back with his crutch but held his rifle.

When all were mounted, the prisoners in between, they rode to the end of the alley where they waited for Ben to give the word. Ben peered into the empty street, but saw no sign of life. He tugged his hat brim down in the sunlight.

"Now," he said.

He dug in his heels and led the wild ride at a full gallop, clattering across the boardwalk and heading across the dusty street toward the saloon.

Hidden on roofs and in alleys, Avery's men opened fire.

Hatcher, kneeling behind a false front over the saloon, laughed as he fired over the galloping posse's heads. He had no intention of hitting the prisoners or Ben Hawks. That was someone else's job. His was sending a message to Pinkley and Posher about what would happen if they blabbed. Besides, he enjoyed making the riders dodge and sway. He scratched under his rawhide vest and swung another shell into his Winchester repeater.

A shot from the jailhouse crashed into the wood next to him. He ducked backward, then swore as one of his big spurs poked him in the rear. Reilly must be firing back, but the marshal could only guess at his targets. Hatcher laughed again, aimed, and pulled the trigger.

Down in the street, men and horses scattered like chickens. Rifle fire cracked, bullets whistling past the posse. One sent Posher's hat sailing. Another struck one of Hack's cowhands in the shoulder. As the riders reached the other side, horses tied nearby jumped and tugged at their reins. The posse and prisoners charged up to the saloon entrance.

Hack's men turned away, leaving the others to duck and ride through the swinging doors. The charging horses skidded on the wooden floor scattering the stacked chairs and sending the few people already in the saloon diving for cover. Luckily, none of the horses fell. Ben pulled his mount up sharply and slid from the saddle. "All yours, Mr. Loophole," he said.

Loophole helped Pinkley and Posher dismount and herded them inside toward the storeroom. Ben left Hack guarding the storeroom door while he helped Sloan and the others take the horses back outside. Then he moved through the gathering crowd with his rifle, watching the roofs and alleys, heading toward the jail. Reilly waited there, watching from the doorway and leaning on a crutch. Four armed deputies lingered nearby.

"See where the shots came from?" Ben asked.

"No, but we made 'em back off."

The lawman looked pale, his jaw set like something hurt. "You sure you're up to this trial?" Ben asked.

Reilly nodded, short and sharp. "I'm prosecuting, and you're blamed right I am."

In her hotel room, Vera Kendall was pinning up her hair when a man serving as bailiff knocked on her door and handed her a subpoena. Stunned, she stood there like a fool and gaped at him. "The trial . . . they're going ahead?" she managed to say. "I mean . . . I heard all the noise, gunfire . . . they're saying someone blew up the jail last night . . . I don't see how . . ."

"Ben Hawks and Marshal Reilly held 'em off," the lanky bailiff said. "Lawyer's with the suspects now. They'll want to hear from you, ma'am." He tipped his hat and walked away down the hall, leaving her to stew. Frantic, she paced her room. This wasn't supposed to happen. Brian had promised her the trial wouldn't take place. Yet here she was, minutes away from being called to the witness stand. Not only would Ben Hawks be there, so would Sara Hawks. A double threat.

At length, she throttled her nerves, pinned her hat to her

head, and strode into the hallway. A few yards away, a swarthy, dark-eyed, fierce-looking man in a black shirt and trousers, sporting fancy twin holsters in his gun belt, emerged from his room. He spotted her and smiled. The expression made her think of a snake.

He nodded toward her. "Vera, you haven't changed."

"Nor have you, Señor Dejado."

His chilly smile widened. "Frye told me everything. And Brian knows I'm here."

She drew her black veil down over her face. "Are you sure you can take Ben Hawks?"

"Yes."

"They say he's very fast."

"Not fast enough."

CHAPTER FIFTEEN

The Wagon Wheel Saloon, set up with rows of chairs and a desk for the judge, began to fill with spectators.

In the front row to the right of the judge were Reilly, Hack, and Ben Hawks, Roxanna and Sara seated behind them. Opposite them on the left, the prisoners sat next to Loophole. They were smirking, which bothered Ben. What scheme had that dude of a lawyer cooked up? His head ached, and he guessed he hadn't fully recovered from the explosion. Whatever the lawyer's plan was, it couldn't matter. Pinkley and Posher had done what they'd done, and he and Buckley and Roxanna could prove it.

Soon, there remained standing room only. Armed deputies stood behind the crowd on each side of the swinging doors. The room rumbled, noisy with excitement. The jury, off to the right, consisted of twelve men, some cowmen, others merchants. One of them, Ben noted, was Chandler Strong. When the small, wiry judge entered, the big man serving as bailiff gestured to the jury to stand until the jurist was seated.

The judge nodded at the bailiff, who read out the charges of attempted murder. When he'd finished, the judge cleared his throat and addressed the prisoners. "How do you plead, boys?"

Loophole rose from his seat. "Not guilty, Your Honor."

From there, the trial unfolded pretty much as Ben expected. He, Roxanna, Buckley, and Hack all testified as to what happened at the ridge, with the marshal asking questions from his chair. The jury, led by Chandler Strong, watched the proceedings intently, but Ben couldn't tell from their faces what any of them were thinking.

Reilly called Vera Kendall. She walked slowly up the aisle from somewhere in the rear of the saloon, her face hidden under her heavy black mourning veil. Ben turned to watch her and caught a whiff of roses as she walked by. Something about her gave him a strange feeling, but he wasn't sure why.

On the stand, Reilly quizzed her. "Mrs. Kendall, prior to the incident at the ridge, were you aware that a Larabee hand named Rossiter had already been killed?"

"Yes," she whispered.

"Your Honor," Loophole protested. "Rossiter's death is irrelevant and immaterial."

The judge leaned forward. "Marshal?"

"Your Honor, what happened to Rossiter was about to happen to Mr. Buckley and Miss Larabee. It ties in to an obvious conspiracy in the Lazy K's ongoing feud with the Crooked Spur."

"I'll allow it. Overruled, Mr. Loophole."

Reilly continued to question Vera. "How long have Pinkley and Posher worked for the Lazy K? Did they hire on recent, and if so, who hired them?"

"I don't know." Her voice remained barely audible. "My late husband Laird and my brother-in-law, Miles Kendall, took care of things like that. I don't know anything about the goings-on between our ranch and the Crooked Spur, either."

"You have no idea who hired the two defendants, and what they were doing on Larabee property?"

"No. No idea at all."

Clearly baffled, Reilly gave up. Loophole had no questions for the widow. When the judge excused her, she hurried down the aisle and left the courtroom.

Ben turned in his chair and watched her leave. His odd, unsettled feeling intensified.

Loophole rose and called Posher to the stand. The defendant admitted being out near the ridge on the day in question, but after that the lies came thick and fast. "We'd been out hunting, and they throwed down on us."

"You didn't fire the first shot?" Loophole asked.

"Heck, no. We dived for cover. They had us pinned down, so we shot back."

"So you were only defending yourselves?"

"Yeah, that's right."

Ben clenched his fists in frustration. The jury couldn't believe that load of bull, could they? Reilly went after Posher on cross exam, but he couldn't change the man's story, nor could he get the defendant Pinkley to weaken his. "Saturday night, someone shot up the jailhouse," Reilly said. "I took four bullets, and two deputies were killed. You boys were in my jail at the time. What do you know about it?"

Loophole rose. "Your Honor, these unfortunate events have nothing to do with my clients. They're immaterial to this trial."

"The heck they are," Reilly shot back. "Someone attacked my jailhouse, then tried to blow it up Sunday night—"

The judge cut him off. "I'm sorry, Marshal Reilly. Unless the defendants had knowledge of or were involved, these incidents have no bearing on the matter at hand." He glanced at the jury, some of whom looked worried. "The jury will disregard them."

When the trial was over, the jury went into the storeroom to confer, and the judge went to the saloon office to wait. The crowd grew restless and noisy.

Ben turned to look at Roxanna and his mother. "What do you think?"

Sara frowned. "It's fifty-fifty."

"Chandler's on the jury," Roxanna said. "He'll believe us."

Within a half hour, the jury and judge returned. Chandler Strong stood up, smoothed the lapels of his fancy frock coat, and drew his hand over his curly brown hair. "Your Honor, we find the defendants not guilty."

The saloon erupted. Posher and Pinkley, standing with Loophole, grinned from ear to ear. The judge pounded his gavel until the noisy spectators fell silent. For a long moment, the judge stared at the jury as if he meant to say something about the verdict. Finally, he turned to Reilly. "Marshal, release the prisoners."

Roxanna's face burned with hot color. Buckley shook his head in dismay. Hack and Reilly looked as furious as Ben felt. Reilly gave the keys to Ben, who swallowed his anger as he went over and removed the handcuffs.

Loophole sauntered to the weary Reilly and offered his hand, which the lawman shook reluctantly. "I'll be seeing you, Marshal," Loophole said.

Reilly grimaced. "You did your job, all right."

Loophole shrugged. "Both sides gave believable testimony, but it was too even. Otherwise, the judge would have taken the verdict away from the jury. My clients simply looked like the helpless, innocent men they are."

Reilly scowled. "You made sure of that."

The defendants left with the crowd, and Loophole turned to follow. Ben remained standing with Reilly, Hack, Buckley, and the women. Everyone else was gone except Chandler Strong.

"The lawyer was right," Chandler said to them.

Roxanna looked furious and hurt. "Didn't you believe us, Chandler?"

"Of course I did, but it was your word against theirs."

"So you went along with it."

"I had no choice, Roxanna." He offered her his arm. "May I escort you out of here?"

"No, thank you," she said, looking away.

Hack's face turned dark red. "You get out of here, Chandler. I don't want to see you around my niece, ever again. You're nothing but a dude in fancy clothes, and you ain't got no guts. You could have made a difference with the rest of the jury, but you're just a pansy."

"I did what I thought was right."

"Well, do it somewhere else, and stay away from the Crooked Spur."

For a moment, Chandler looked dismayed. Then he managed a smile, bowed to the ladies, turned, and left the courtroom.

Reilly sat dangling the handcuff keys from his fingers. He looked exhausted and in pain. Hack, sitting near him, shook his head. Roxanna got to her feet, so angry she couldn't speak.

Sara turned to Reilly. "You did your best, Marshal. Now what about the men who tried to bust them out? And the ones who tried to kill them? Why aren't they in jail?"

Reilly grunted, clasping the keys in his hand as if to hand them over. "You want the job?"

Sara made a face. "Don't get smart with me. I'm just trying to get you to focus on what's important. Somebody was trying to shut those two boys up. Now maybe it was that widow woman, since her menfolk likely set it all up. I wonder what she looks like under all that black veil."

"A right pretty woman," Reilly said.

There wasn't much else to say, and soon afterward, the group broke up. Hack stayed with Reilly, and the women walked with Ben back toward the hotel. Most of the crowd had moved into saloons and stores to talk about the big trial. Some had charged back into the Wagon Wheel to get it going, and the piano was already playing a lively tune.

Over a noonday meal in the hotel restaurant with his mother and Roxanna, Ben sat staring into his coffee. His head hurt again, and the rest of him didn't feel much better.

"Son, are you all right?" Sara asked.

"Nothing makes sense anymore," Ben said.

Sara stabbed a potato with her fork. "It's a bad day, that's certain."

Roxanna looked at Ben. "What will you do now?"

Ben clasped his hands around his coffee cup. "I don't know."

Sara leaned toward her son. "You could leave town before that killer Dejado gets around to putting on his show."

"You want me to run?"

"Not talking about running," Sara said, clearly miffed.

"Ben Hawks has no sense," Roxanna said.

Sara smiled at her. "Why Hack ever let that dandy Strong hang around you, I'll never know. I would have run him off with a shotgun."

Chandler Strong wasn't thinking about Roxanna as he entered Vera's hotel room that evening with Frye on his heels. The heavy curtains were drawn, and the lamp burned bright. Vera sat in a chair near the dressing table, composed, hands in her lap. The men removed their hats and stood near the door, facing her. They spoke quietly, but Frye looked jubilant. "We won hands down today," he said.

Chandler nodded. "I'll keep that lawyer in mind. We may need him again."

"I don't understand it," Vera said, "and I'm glad it's over. But can you trust Posher and Pinkley now?"

"We had them scared silly," Chandler said. "I gave them money and told them to get over to Little Bend and lay low."

She made a face. "What about the Larabees?"

"I'm not welcome out there anymore. If we still want the Crooked Spur, we'll have to get rid of them both."

"And Ben Hawks," she added.

141

"You'd better see to the men," Chandler said to Frye, who reluctantly left.

Vera stood and moved toward Chandler. He held her and kissed her platinum blonde hair. "Please," she whispered as he embraced her, "you have to get rid of Ben Hawks."

"Dejado will take care of him."

And he kissed her into silence.

CHAPTER SIXTEEN

Early the next morning, the Larabee hands brought the horses, including Ben's gelding, and a wagon to the hotel. Sara and Roxanna stood at the hotel entrance with their luggage while a grim-faced Sloan and the hands loaded up supplies for the Crooked Spur. The wind was rising and the smell of rain hung in the chilly air.

Buckley joined Roxanna and Sara, tipping his hat to them. "Some of the store owners are getting up money to rebuild the jail. Posher and Pinkley left town in a hurry. That fellow Dejado's having breakfast at the saloon. And Frye's over at the livery with his men."

"And my son?" Sara asked.

"He's with Mr. Larabee and the marshal, in the jail," Buckley said.

The windmill noisily turned near the church as dust blew down the street. A tumbleweed came spinning from the alley by the Wagon Wheel, skipped across the distance to the jail, and slammed against the hitching post where it bounced a little now and then.

After a short while, Reilly, Ben, and Hack came out of the jail. The marshal still hobbled on his crutch. He nodded toward the Wagon Wheel. Hack and Ben turned to follow his gaze.

A lone man came out of the saloon and leaned on a post. He puffed on a smoke. Clad all in black, with fancy twin holsters and a fierce, sneering face, he looked more than dangerous.

He fixed his hard eyes on Ben and slowly straightened. Watching him, Roxanna felt a deep chill that had nothing to do with the wind.

"Dejado," Reilly muttered.

Ben looked around. A crowd had gathered in doorways and windows. He could see Frye and some others standing just out of the wind, at the express office entrance. His gaze went back to the black-clad gunslinger and stayed there.

"You don't have to do this, Ben," Reilly said.

"That's so," Hack agreed.

"I'll run him out of town," Reilly growled. "I'll get my shotgun."

Ben felt his stomach turning into a rock. "You'd just get yourself killed." Everyone knew Dejado was the fastest gun alive. Ben remembered Roxanna's words when they first met: *Don't you know somebody's going to be faster than you? You're going to Boot Hill at a full gallop, and you don't even know it.*

He felt cold sweat forming on his back. "Could be Avery's paying him. I aim to find out."

Ben loosened his bandanna. Dejado moved into the street some twenty paces up as drizzle began falling.

Ben drew a deep breath. Dejado just might lead him to Avery. Ben's three-year hunt could end this dreary morning, one way or another. Painfully, he realized he had more reason to live than he'd ever had. Along with his feisty mother, he had a friend in Reilly, a father figure in Hack, and hope of a future that might include Roxanna. His resolve had lessened, and that could be dangerous in facing a killer.

He moved into the street as he tugged his hat down tight. The rain made Dejado's crazy black eyes look even darker in his fierce face. Around them, Ben sensed men peering from cover along the boardwalks on both sides of the street. He was dimly aware of Roxanna and Sara, watching from the hotel entrance just out of the rain.

Dejado dropped his smoke to the ground. "Hawks."

Ben stayed still. "I've got no cause to fight you, Dejado."

"Because you're yellow?"

"Because I'm here looking for Brian Avery and his men. Unless you're one of them, I got no fight with you."

"Oh, yes, the Tucson stage robbery. You went loco after that."

"You were there?"

"I was in prison when it happened."

"Don't mean you ain't one of 'em."

"You're trying to talk your way out of this, Hawks, and it's not going to happen. When I'm ready, you're going to die."

"You know who Avery is?"

"I might. But you're going to have to draw on me to find out."

Ben swallowed hard, his mouth dry, his arms heavy at his sides. He hadn't been practicing of late. He'd gotten lucky with Pecos. He wasn't sure his luck was going to hold.

Dejado waited. No one moved.

Cold to his boots and stiff, Ben had never felt so unprepared. Dejado looked calculating, deadly, ready to draw.

"Afraid?" Dejado sneered.

"I'm not going to draw," Ben said.

Dejado drew, fast and sure. Instinct took over, and Ben's Colt leaped into his right hand. Even as the gunman pulled the trigger, Ben's shot slammed into the man's chest. Dejado's bullet whistled by Ben's ear.

Lowering his weapon, Ben stared as the gunman dropped to his knees and his six-gun landed in the street. Ben had meant only to wound, but his well-honed reflexes had other ideas. He moved forward slowly, heart pounding. He paused in front of the gunman, who stared up at him.

"Avery pay you?" Ben demanded.

Dejado nodded, pressing one hand against the bloody hole in his chest.

"Who is he?"

The gunman's mouth moved, but no sound came forth.

"Is Avery here?" Ben persisted.

Dejado nodded. He swayed, eyes turned upward, and tried to make the sign of the cross on his chest. Then he fell forward, face down in the dirt.

Ben knelt and turned him on his side. "Who's Avery?"

No answer came. The man was dead.

Agony crawled through Ben as he got to his feet a little too fast. He turned to look at the gathering crowd, their faces swimming before him. A bitter sense of failure added to his physical pain. If he hadn't shot so fast, had aimed for Dejado's shoulder or someplace else less swiftly fatal . . .

Dazed, he stumbled as he turned. Hack rushed to his side and caught his arm. "Come along, Ben."

The rancher marched him out of the street and back inside the jail.

Reilly tried to bar the door, but Sara shoved her way inside. She hurried to help Ben to a chair and sat next to him. Hack gave him coffee. He had trouble holding the cup in both hands. Sara steadied it for him, and he took a sip.

"Were you hit?" Reilly asked from where he sat on the cot.

"No," Ben said, "but I guess I'm still rocky from the dynamite. I stood up too quick."

Hack nodded as he pulled up a chair. "Ben, I never saw anyone so fast."

"Avery's gonna have to get you in the back," Reilly said. "Maybe it's time you gave up and went on back to Texas."

"Where's Roxanna?" Hack asked.

"Back at the hotel," Sara said. "She was very upset." She watched her son closely, noting the dismay that crossed his face at the mention of Roxanna's name. Ben seemed to care for this girl, and Roxanna clearly cared for him. Suddenly overwhelmed by her own emotion, Sara poured Ben more coffee and dabbed at a tear on her cheek.

"Maybe you're just guessing, Ben," Hack said. "Dejado said as how Avery paid him, but it doesn't mean Avery is here."

Reilly nodded. "He could have been lying." The marshal fussed with the bandage under his own shirt. He looked exhausted.

"Ben, are you all right now?" Sara asked.

He sipped coffee and nodded.

Hack stirred. "I can take you back to the hotel, ma'am. You look wrung out, if you don't mind my saying so."

Sara drew herself up. "I do mind. And I'm not leaving."

"It'd maybe do your son good not to be worrying about you," Hack said.

Sara gazed at him for a long moment. He'd spoken more gently than he usually did, from what she'd observed of him. Deciding she'd won this round, she stood up and leaned over to kiss Ben's cheek. "You stay put, son, or I'll tan your hide."

Hack tried to frown, but made a poor job of it as he escorted her to the door. A man with some humor to him, Sara thought. Maybe this rough-edged rancher wasn't such a bad sort after all.

Vera Kendall sat in the hotel restaurant, having a late breakfast with Chandler Strong. She felt too anxious to enjoy it much, though. They made small talk until the old serving man vanished into the back and they were alone in the small dining room. Vera sighed as she adjusted her veil. "Maybe no one can kill Ben Hawks."

Chandler reached over and laid his hand on hers. "You're trembling."

"I'm afraid."

"We don't have to get Hawks face on."

She frowned at him. "What about his mother?"

"When Hawks is dead, won't be no need for her to stick around. Just stay away from her."

She turned her hand to clasp his and smiled, then looked past him. She tensed and stared at her plate. "She's coming. Roxanna's coming."

He continued to hold her hand as Roxanna came walking up in her riding outfit and flowing skirts, her lustrous hair falling about her face as she gazed at them. "Am I interrupting?"

"I was just comforting Mrs. Kendall. Please, sit down."

He released Vera's hand and stood up to pull a chair around for Roxanna, but she remained standing, a stony expression on her face.

Vera peered at her through the dark veil. "What is it you want, Miss Larabee?"

"I think you know more than you're telling. I think Rossiter was killed to shut him up. And the Kendalls were murdered so you'd have the ranch."

Vera shook her head. "I'm in mourning. Have you no respect?"

"I think you lied at the trial."

"Please get out of here, Miss Larabee, before I forget I'm a lady."

"I think you forgot that a long time ago."

Rage flared inside Vera, barely controlled. "How dare you!"

"I see right through you," Roxanna said. "If anything happens to Ben Hawks, I'm coming after you myself."

"Miss Roxanna," Chandler said, "you're just worried for no reason."

"I trusted you," Roxanna snapped at him.

"I'm sorry," he said. "I'll try to earn it back."

"Don't bother." Roxanna spun on her heel and left.

Chandler sat down. Vera kicked him under the table.

"Ow. What'd you do that for?"

"You like her a little too much."

Roxanna charged back into the lobby, where she met Uncle Hack and Sara Hawks coming through the front door.

"Roxanna, what's wrong?" Hack asked.

"Nothing I couldn't fix with a well-placed bullet."

Sara Hawks laughed. "A girl after my own heart. Come along upstairs. We'll get some rest and have some female conversation."

"Doesn't work for me," Hack said.

"You're not invited," Sara snapped, but her eyes twinkled.

Hack grinned down at her, tipped his hat, and left.

"You like my uncle," Roxanna said as they went up the stairs.

"And you like my Ben."

CHAPTER SEVENTEEN

In the jailhouse, with clouds drifting past the sun outside, Ben sat in his chair feeling stiff and cold. Relief at surviving the shootout with Dejado mixed with dread at the knowledge that now he was far more likely to be shot in the back.

As Ben watched Hack, who stood by the stove making fresh coffee, he no longer believed Hack could also be Brian Avery. The rancher was like no one Ben had ever met, but he had more honor than a man like Avery could ever claim.

A knock at the door brought a Crooked Spur ranch hand with a letter for Reilly. After the ranch hand left, Reilly opened the letter and read it.

At length, Reilly waved the letter at Ben and Hack. "This came from Texas. Says here some fellows was headed this way a while back. One of 'em's called Tinsley. They suspect he used to ride with Avery. Did some bragging when he was drunk, but his face ain't on no handbills. They don't know the other fellow's name."

"Did they say what he looks like?"

Reilly frowned. "Not much. They only saw him the once, riding out of town with Tinsley. Tall, they figured, but nothing particular else about him. Not fat or real skinny, no distinguishing marks. Couldn't even be sure what color his hair is, under his hat."

Another knock came at the door. Hack went over and let Sloan inside. The foreman went to the stove and helped himself

150

to the thick coffee.

Reilly held up the letter. "Sloan, you know any fellow named Tinsley?"

"Yeah, sure. Played cards with him and a friend of his, some fellow named Brownie. They're over at the Wagon Wheel right now, as a matter of fact."

"We think he rode with Avery," Reilly said.

Ben got to his feet and drew his six-guns one at a time to check the load.

Reilly gave him a stern look. "Ben, I'm the law around here. I'll go into the saloon. Besides, you still don't have your head on straight."

"Better shape than you," Ben said. "You don't see me with no crutch."

Reilly grunted. "You want to help, Ben, you come in from the back."

"What about me and Sloan?" Hack asked.

"Soon's we move on Tinsley," Reilly said, "some other rats might try to get away. The two of you can get out there on the boardwalk and keep an eye out. And don't let the judge leave on that stage when it gets here."

"It'll be late," Hack said. "Always is."

"What does Tinsley look like?" Reilly asked.

Sloan made a face. "Short and ugly. Got curly hair."

"And Brownie?"

"Husky. Rough face. Square jaw, sticks out," Sloan said. "They was playing cards on the left side as you go in, away from the piano player. Tinsley had his back to the wall. Brownie was facing the door."

Reilly got up. He ignored his crutch as he reached for his shotgun and checked the load. "Let's go."

Ben unbarred the door and opened it. The sky had darkened with fast-moving clouds. The wind blew the dust and sent tumbleweeds into a spin. Damp air promised rain, and on the far eastern horizon over the foothills, lightning flashed.

"We want 'em alive," Ben said.

Leaving his crutch behind and carrying his shotgun, Reilly hobbled onto the boardwalk with him. Sloan and Hack followed at a distance. Ben moved ahead toward the alley, left of the saloon. Sprinkling rain began to fall, spitting the dust around them.

As he moved through the alley and around the back of the saloon, Ben felt sweat break out all over him. He didn't know if Tinsley was Avery, or if Brownie was, or if Avery was even in these parts. Dejado could have lied, or Avery could have been here and left.

He reached the saloon and eased open the back door. As silently as he could, he drew his right-hand Colt and moved into the rear hallway, stepping over the pail and mop, avoiding the boxes and pans. He passed the door to the storeroom and reached the one to the main room. Slowly, he turned the knob and pushed it open.

The piano stood silent. The fat barkeep, at the far end of the walnut bar, wiped glasses as he talked to an old man. The only other customers were the two men at a table by the wall on the left side of the room with a bottle of whiskey between them. The fellow dealing cards matched Sloan's description of Tinsley. The huskier man with his back to Ben must be Brownie. Both men wore iron and looked like they knew how to use it.

Ben swallowed and waited. He spared a moment's worry for Reilly out front, hobbling toward the swinging doors.

Tinsley and Brownie were talking, their voices too low for Ben to hear what they said. Abruptly, Brownie slammed his cards down. "You're cheating again, Tinsley."

"No more'n you."

"Let me see your sleeves."

"Let me see yours, dag nab it."

"Just like in Tucson. You ain't changed."

"Yeah, well, you ain't got no smarter."

Then the two men laughed and Brownie took the cards, shuffling them with a snort. Tinsley poured whiskey for both of them.

Reilly pushed through the swinging doors and entered the saloon. To Ben's surprise, Hack was a step behind him. Taking his cue, Ben moved forward.

Tinsley stared at Reilly and Hack. He set the bottle down and slipped his right hand under the table out of sight. Brownie gripped the table's edge.

"Hands where I can see 'em, Tinsley," Reilly said.

"Now," Ben ordered.

Tinsley froze, then brought his right hand back up and rested both hands on the tabletop. "We ain't done nothing."

"Stand up, both of you," Reilly said. "Reach for the ceiling."

The two men slowly got to their feet. "What for?" Brownie demanded.

"You're wanted for riding with the Avery gang."

Tinsley grabbed for his gun. Brownie spun as he reached for his.

Reilly's shotgun blasted. The impact threw Tinsley against the wall, his six-gun sailing into the air. Ben cursed, and holstered his own six-gun as Brownie's gun cleared leather. Determined to keep the man alive, Ben charged him. Brownie's shot went wild as Ben crashed into him, sent his weapon flying, and knocked him backward onto the table.

Brownie was powerful as a bull, and Ben couldn't hold him down. He roared upward and slammed his fist into Ben's face. Ben shook off the blow, grabbed him by the shirt, and swung him into the wall, then charged again. The big man grabbed for Ben's throat, but Ben ducked and rammed his right fist into the man's gut. As Brownie gasped and doubled over, Ben caught him on the jaw with a left uppercut. Brownie pulled him into a bear hug. Ben fought for air, then slammed his fist into Brownie's nose.

The big man hollered and let go of Ben. He shook his head, blood spurting. Ben let him drop to one knee as Reilly came close with his shotgun.

"I got another load in here," the lawman said.

Brownie, breathing hard, looked at the dead Tinsley, who lay in a blood-covered heap. "I'm done," Brownie said.

Reilly waved his shotgun. "All right, march."

Brownie clumsily got to his feet as Hack cuffed him behind his back. The bartender and the old man poked their heads up from behind the bar, watching cautiously.

"You both rode with Avery," Ben said, hoping to trap Brownie.

"I ain't never heard of no Avery."

"Tinsley was one of Avery's gang, and you're Tinsley's partner."

"I hardly knew Tinsley."

"I heard you talking about being together in Tucson," Ben said.

"You're loco."

Reilly poked at Brownie with his shotgun. "Let's go."

They marched him out of the saloon and across the street through a gathering crowd that fell back to give them room. Ben limped from the exertion, and Hack came up beside him as they headed for the jail. Sloan walked ahead of them and opened the jailhouse door, then stood aside.

With no cells, Reilly settled for seating Brownie on the floor with his back against a wall. Brownie cussed under his breath and glared at them with beady eyes. Sloan left to find the judge and Hack barred the door, while Ben sat down to rest.

"Now then, Brownie," Reilly said as he sat down on his cot.

"Let's hear your story."

Sullen, the man scowled at him. "I ain't done nothing."

"You were in on that stage robbery in '76, this side of Tucson," Ben snapped. "You and Avery and the others left everyone dead. And you took the largest bank shipment ever stolen."

"I ain't done no such thing."

"And now Avery has to shut you up."

"Hah. How do you know I ain't Avery?"

"Because you ain't smart enough."

"Avery never made a move without asking my . . ." Brownie's smug look vanished as he caught himself. He drew back against the wall, glaring at them.

Ben felt weak and drained, his heart heavy with years of waiting. He was so close and yet so far from getting Avery. He had to shake something loose. "How big was your share of the loot from Tucson? Avery cheat you? I bet he kept the most for himself—"

Sudden pounding at the door cut him off. Hack walked over and opened it a crack, then frowned. "You ain't welcome here. Git."

"I have official business. Let me in." The voice was Loophole's. Making a face, Hack unbarred the door and allowed the lawyer inside.

Reilly grunted from his cot. "You got here awful fast."

"I was hired to defend this man."

"Who hired you?"

"That's confidential," Loophole said.

Hack spoke up. "Seems to me you're pushing your luck."

Loophole eyed him like he smelled bad. "I will not reveal the name of the good citizen who put up the money to defend this poor, wretched soul."

"Hey," Brownie said. "I ain't no wretch."

"Marshal, I'd like to be alone with my client."

"Well, now," Reilly drawled, "we ain't got no way to do that. Not until we get him over to the saloon for trial. Which we will be holding as soon as we locate the judge."

Loophole drew himself up. "Then my client will have nothing to say from now on."

"He's already as much as admitted he rode with Avery," Reilly said.

"Is that all you have? A frightened man's confusion?" Loophole smiled. "This will be an easy job for me. No jury will convict him on something he will deny having said."

"He resisted arrest," the lawman said.

"After you came at him with a shotgun."

Ben jumped in. "Word traveled fast, did it?"

"We got enough to hold him until we check out his story," Reilly snapped back.

"Very well. A preliminary hearing might be in order. Let's see what the judge says about whether you have enough evidence. I'll ask him to hold court this afternoon."

Brownie chuckled. "That's telling you, Marshal."

The lawyer looked down at him, frowning, then turned away and let himself out. "I'll keep an eye on him," Hack said, and followed.

Ben leaned back in his chair and picked up his cup. For the first time since the gunfight with Dejado, he let himself relax enough to savor the hot coffee. Reilly, still weary from his wounds, lay down on his cot and closed his eyes.

Ben had to admire the lawman's strength and endurance. He felt just about at the end of his rope.

Two hours later, Ben and Reilly brought their prisoner to the saloon. The hearing would be brief, so no one had bothered setting the Wagon Wheel up for court.

Loophole got his time with Brownie, and then they all stood waiting for the judge. A dozen or so men crowded into the back of the room, but there were no chairs set up and no other spectators.

The judge came in from the back door, papers in hand, and seated himself at the table nearest to Brownie, Loophole, Reilly, and Ben. He shuffled the papers, not looking up. "Well, Marshal Reilly? What's this about?"

"Your Honor," Reilly said, "a short while ago I was forced to shoot dead a fellow named Tinsley when he resisted arrest on these very premises and went for his gun. Tinsley rode with the Avery gang. While playing cards, Tinsley and Brownie here"—he nodded toward the prisoner—"were overheard discussing their time together in Tucson. At the jail a short time later, Brownie as much as admitted he rode with Avery. You recall, Brian Avery and his gang robbed the Tucson stage three years back."

"He sign anything?" the judge asked, making notes.

"No, sir."

"Your Honor," Loophole said, "my client reacted in self-defense. He didn't see it was the marshal. All he saw was a shotgun and his friend being blasted against the wall. He thought his life was in danger."

The judge nodded. "I see. Well, Marshal, if that's all you have—" He looked up and caught sight of Brownie. His eyes narrowed and a grim smile spread across his face. Loophole shifted his weight as the prisoner stared at the judge.

Tapping his pencil on the papers in front of him, the judge leaned back, still smiling.

"Your Honor," Loophole said. "My client—"

"Is Lester T. Brown. Arrested for robbery and attempted murder near Mesilla, four years ago. He was with the Avery gang and was the only one caught. Escaped from jail before trial. My feelings were sorely hurt, Mr. Brown, your leaving that way."

Loophole looked startled, then stood taller. "Your Honor, this court is prejudiced against my client. I respectfully request a change of venue."

The judge put his fingertips together. "Counselor, it was the Avery gang who helped this man escape from Mesilla."

Reilly grinned, and Ben's spirits lifted a bit. Loophole looked beside himself. "Your Honor, the only way my client can receive a fair trial is—"

"If you question the integrity of this court one more time, I'll hold you in contempt. And your client is going back to Mesilla. That's where the witnesses are."

"Yes, Your Honor," Loophole said lamely.

It took Ben a moment to realize this wasn't exactly the outcome he wanted. "Your Honor—"

The judge ignored him. "I'll be on that stage myself. You may accompany him back to Mesilla. Marshal, can you arrange for deputies to escort us?"

"Yes, sir, I sure can."

"Your Honor," Ben said grimly. "This man knows how to find Avery."

The judge nodded. "You're Ben Hawks. I heard about you."

Loophole straightened. "My client would consider immunity for his testimony against Avery."

Brownie gaped at the lawyer. "I ain't talking. I'd be dead before I hit the street."

The judge looked firm. "I can see reduced sentencing for armed robbery in exchange for his testimony if it leads to finding Avery, but the attempted murder charge stands."

Agitated, Ben persisted. "Your Honor, I need time to question this man."

Loophole spoke before the judge could reply. "My client is

not answering any questions. You want to ask him anything, you come to the trial in Mesilla." Turning toward the judge, Loophole asked for time with Brownie again. The two were escorted to the storeroom, with Sloan on guard outside the door.

Furious, Ben looked around at the small crowd inside the saloon, searching for faces that might be Avery or his men. So close to the truth, and yet, where were they?

Chapter Eighteen

Later that day, four of Hack's men were deputized to guard Brownie on his way to Mesilla. The stage came in and took on fresh horses. When it finally headed south with the judge, Loophole and Brownie, Ben watched from the boardwalk in front of the jail. Rain threatened under an even darker sky, matching his grim mood.

Reilly hobbled outside to watch the coach drive away, the big vehicle rocking and bouncing on its leather hinges, the deputies trailing behind it. "Sorry, Ben. I know Brownie could have told you something. One thing for sure, Avery can't get to him with that kind of escort."

"But Avery's got to be here."

"We don't know for sure."

As drizzle began to fall, Ben walked up and down the street, eyeing every man he saw, his stomach churning. He paused after a while and watched the Widow Kendall as she left town with an escort of Frye and seven ranch hands from the Lazy K. Wearing a heavy cape and dark veil while Frye held a large umbrella over her head, she didn't look Ben's way.

Chandler Strong walked up and kissed Vera's hand before she climbed onto the wagon seat. Ben figured the dandy as an opportunist, bound to get the widow and her ranch.

At twilight, with light rain still falling, Ben sat in the jail with Hack and Reilly, playing three-handed poker. Ben had a stack of matches in front of him.

"Reilly, you think he's cheating?" Hack growled.

"If he is, I sure ain't caught 'im."

"I'm from Texas," Ben said. "I don't have to cheat."

"Well, I was born in Texas," Hack said. "Grew up in Missouri."

"And I'm from Ohio," Reilly snapped.

"I sure can't be cheating, Reilly," Hack grumbled. "Or I'd be winning."

"Texans don't cheat," Ben insisted.

Just then, a banging at the door brought Hack to his feet. When he asked who it was, Buckley answered, so he removed the bar to let the young ranch hand in. Sara Hawks followed right behind.

"Why aren't you at the hotel?" Hack asked her.

"You never mind," she said. "I'm here to check on my son."

"He's not so dizzy he doesn't win at poker," Reilly said with a grin.

Sara marched over to where Ben sat. "After Dejado, they'll have to get you in the back," she told him. "I lost your father that way, and I won't lose you." She moved closer to him and laid a hand on his shoulder. "I'm telling you, it's time you gave up and went on back to Texas."

Despite being a seasoned gunslinger and former ranger, Ben always felt like a small boy when his mother fussed over him. He tried to maintain his determination, but she could turn his insides into mush. He patted her hand, knowing she would read the discomfort in his face, unable to say a word in his own defense.

Hack came to his rescue. "Where's Roxanna?"

Sara frowned as if puzzled. "At the hotel. Why?"

"You go check on her," Hack said. "Me and Reilly, we'll look after Ben and try to talk some sense into him."

"There you go again," Sara said. "You're still ordering me around, and I won't have it."

Hack squared his shoulders with a grin. "I sort of enjoy it."

Her chin went up a little, but she smiled and headed for the door.

"Buckley," Hack said, "keep an eye on these women."

Buckley grinned as he and Sara walked out into the twilight.

Back at the hotel as the rain stopped and night fell, Roxanna huddled in a chair in the empty lobby. She felt miserable, gripping the jacket of her blue silk dress with icy fingers. She couldn't move until someone prodded her. "You look like a wet Monday," Sara Hawks said, shrugging out of her cape. "Let me buy you supper and we'll talk."

Too anxious to object, Roxanna followed Ben's mother into the hotel dining room. The two of them shared a table away from the dozen men who were eating nearby. Lamplight danced across the room. Roxanna felt a bit better, though not much, as she ate what she could of the fried chicken and potatoes Sara ordered for them. After they finished their meal, she sipped gratefully at the hot coffee the ancient waiter brought.

"Someone hired Dejado," Roxanna said, after the old man moved off toward other guests.

"And now they know they can't take Ben in a fair fight."

Roxanna winced. "They'll ambush him."

"I reckon it's time he forgot about Lora Bedloe and started over. You're full of spit and vinegar. You just might be all right for him."

Roxanna had to smile as she sniffed back a tear. "He doesn't like me very much."

"He's just scared of you," Sara said.

Roxanna used her napkin to wipe her eyes. Sara sipped her coffee. "And you're a lot prettier than Lora was."

"Really?" She felt foolish, setting store by a compliment when Ben was in such danger, but she couldn't help it.

"Sure, take a look." Sara fumbled in her belt purse. "I've had this locket ever since they sent it to Ben after Lora died. He gave it to me to keep for him."

"He really loved her, I guess."

"Ben was just a hard-riding young ranger who never had nothing to do with women. Then she came on the stagecoach and went after him with all that sweet charm. I didn't trust her, but I kept my mouth shut. Smitten men don't listen to their mothers. She swallowed him up, like a rattler with a bird."

At length, Sara found the locket and drew it out. Shiny gold, it dangled on a gold chain. She handed it to Roxanna, who struggled to open it. The grumpy old waiter came to refill their coffee cups.

Finally, Roxanna opened the locket. She stared at the miniature portraits of Ben and Lora.

"I don't understand," Roxanna breathed. "It's Vera Kendall."

The waiter slopped coffee on the table. Scowling, he grunted an apology and mopped up with Sara's napkin, then walked away and vanished someplace in the back.

"What are you saying?" Sara whispered.

Roxanna kept her own voice low as well. "Vera has blonde hair, not dark brown, but I'd know that face anywhere."

Sara gripped Roxanna's wrist. "Are you trying to tell me Lora's alive?"

"Yes. This is Vera Kendall."

"It can't be."

Roxanna glanced up at Sara, her mind working swiftly. "You said none of the bodies from the Tucson stage robbery could be identified."

"Maybe Lora has a twin?" Sara said. "The Kendall woman and that Harry Frye left town this afternoon. I guess they went back to their ranch."

Roxanna snapped the locket shut. "My uncle will verify this is Vera Kendall."

"They're at the jail." Sara grabbed her cape off the back of her chair. "Let's go."

Roxanna had regained her energy. She threw her own cape around her shoulders and jumped up from her chair, leading the way. Sara tossed money on the table and followed her out into the cold night.

The waiter tapped on the door of Chandler Strong's room. When the door opened, he pushed his way inside. Chandler frowned. "What do you want?"

"You said if I ever heard anything interesting, you'd pay me."

"All right, what is it?"

"That Sara Hawks and Miss Larabee, they were having supper. The Hawks woman pulls out a locket. Ben Hawks and his sweetheart got their faces in it. But Miss Larabee, she says it's Vera Kendall in there."

Chandler drew a deep breath. He reached inside his coat, drew out a greenback, and shoved it into the old man's hand. "Keep it to yourself." He herded the old man out and closed the door.

Under a gloomy night sky with street lamps flickering, Sara and Roxanna hurried up the boardwalk in the cold. A half-moon peeked out from behind a bank of dark clouds.

"I'm afraid to tell him," Roxanna whispered.

"It's got to be done."

They reached the jail and stood a moment, looking at the lamplight seeping through the front shutters.

"I don't want to hurt him," Roxanna said.

Sara patted her arm. "We're saving him."

Roxanna shivered under her cape as Sara went up to pound on the door.

CHAPTER NINETEEN

Inside the jail, Reilly, Hack, and Ben sat around with lamps low, telling stories to keep tension at bay.

"My turn." Ben sipped coffee, glad of the hot drink in the chilly jailhouse. "You ever hear the one about Bigfoot Wallace and the ambush at Devil River? Well, back in 1850 or so, when Wallace ran the mail coach from San Antonio to El Paso, there was this place along the Devil River, surrounded by bluffs—big high ones, a perfect spot for a Comanche attack—"

A knock at the door cut him off. Ben exchanged glances with Reilly and Hack. Then Hack shrugged. "Mighty cold night for sending trouble our way," he said as he got up and opened the door. A frown crossed his face as Sara and Roxanna forced their way inside. When they dropped their hoods back, Ben saw their grim, flushed faces and felt a fresh jolt of worry.

Before he could speak, Hack growled, "What're you doing here? You women shouldn't be out on the street at night."

"Hack's right," Reilly said. "You both should have stayed at the hotel."

"They could use either one of you to get at Ben," Hack warned as Ben motioned both women to chairs and seated himself between them.

Ben turned to his mother. He knew that look on her face, a mix of anger and sorrow. Something had upset her, something more than mere knowledge of the peril he was in. His gaze went to her clenched fist resting on the table. "Ma? What is it?"

Sara opened her hand. A familiar locket lay in her palm, gleaming in the lamplight. "Son, do you remember this?"

Uneasy, Ben nodded. For three years he had avoided it, tried not to remember what would cause him more pain than he could bear. He looked away, refusing to touch the thing. Whatever was making his mother show it to him now, he wanted no part of.

Sara eyed him for a long moment, then handed the locket to Hack. "Take a look inside. Tell me what you see."

Hack had trouble opening the locket. Ben kept his attention on his coffee while everyone else watched and waited.

Then Hack caught his breath. "I don't understand. That's Vera Kendall."

Shock robbed Ben of his senses. His heart turned hard as a stone; his mind stopped working. He sat there as if he had died, a hunk of flesh that couldn't move. He could scarcely grasp what craziness he'd heard, and he didn't want to know how it could be true. Lora, alive. His recurring dream. Yet she was someone else. Impossible.

"It's Vera Kendall, all right," Reilly said as Hack showed him the locket. "Dark hair instead of yellow, but it's her. What does this mean?"

Sara's anger brought hot color to her cheeks. "It means Lora Bedloe was a phony. She worked on Ben to help her get that job with the express company so she could learn all about that big bank shipment. She was in it with Avery."

"Didn't Lora Bedloe die in the wreck?" Reilly asked. "If it wasn't her, then who was the woman on the stagecoach?"

Sara shook her head. "Had to be someone she tricked into traveling on her pass."

"Right cold-blooded," Reilly said. "If the stage hadn't crashed, they would have had to make sure the woman could never be recognized."

Sara looked fierce. "And now Lora, or whoever, is here and got herself a ranch after getting both the Kendall brothers shot dead."

Reilly grimaced. "If she was in on it with Avery, then Ben's right about his being somewhere around here, orchestrating everything."

Ben stared at his hands as he tried to squeeze his cup to pieces. He didn't want to believe what he heard. Everything inside of him churned like hot butter. And yet he remembered his first reaction at Lora's grave three years ago, that she wasn't buried there.

"So Lora Bedloe never existed?" Hack asked.

"No," Sara replied. "This Vera, whoever she is, made it all up. She said yes to my son and never meant a word of it."

Ben's face burned hot. His heart felt like stone. He knew he couldn't be the only man fooled by a woman. He knew others must have lost their way in the face of love. Yet it didn't help. Bitter and driven as he'd been in the past, the truth made it far worse. He thought of the men he'd killed in his quest for revenge against Avery, and a pang of remorse shot through him. Right now it was more than he could handle.

Hack laid a hand on his shoulder. "It happens to a lot of men. I'm sorry, son."

"I always thought her hair was too perfect," Sara said. "Never even blew in the wind. I'll bet anything it was a wig."

Roxanna reached over and laid her hand on Ben's. "You had no way of knowing."

Reilly scowled. "Dirty business, if it's true."

"It is true." Sara caught Roxanna's eye. "That locket with Lora's picture was her gift to Ben. Miss Larabee knows Vera Kendall, and so do you and Mr. Larabee. Unless you're going to tell me they're twins?"

"Vera's pretty new in these parts," Hack said slowly. "What

was it, just four months ago Laird Kendall married her? And he met her off the stagecoach . . ."

Sara sat up straighter. "There's one way to find out if she's who we think she is. We'll go to the ranch and confront her."

"You're not going anywhere," Hack said. "If she is Avery's woman, she's surrounded by killers. Does anyone else know about this?"

Sara leaned back in thought. "Yes, the waiter at the hotel. He was standing there when Roxanna recognized the portrait."

"He's just an old man," Reilly said. "He's been around here a long time. Got family. I don't think he's got any connection with Avery."

"So now what?" Hack asked as Reilly returned the locket to Sara.

Sara glanced at Ben, who shook his head and looked away. Three lonely years of hunting Lora's killers, nights on the trail, days of vengeance unsatisfied, and all for a woman who never existed. If it was true. But it couldn't be. It couldn't.

Sara closed the locket.

"First thing in the morning," Reilly said, "I'll go have a talk with Mrs. Kendall."

"You ain't that recovered," Hack warned. "I doubt you could sit a saddle."

Reilly grimaced. "I'm going."

"So am I," Hack said.

Sara frowned. "You charge out there with this, they'll kill you."

Ben leaned forward in his chair, his face pale, his voice strained. "I'm the only one who'll know for sure if Vera Kendall is Lora Bedloe."

"We'll all go," Hack said. "First light."

"But no women," Reilly added, ignoring Sara's glare. "No

169

telling what we'll run into out there."

Hack nodded. "I'll escort the ladies back to the hotel."

Ben chose to sleep in the jailhouse that night, on a bunk salvaged from the cells. He didn't want to be alone. Having Reilly nearby gave him some comfort.

As Ben lay back in the lamplight, he felt plumb miserable.

From his cot where he lay on his side, Reilly spoke softly. "If it'll help, Ben, the driver of that coach had a wife and nine children under fourteen."

It helped a great deal, easing Ben's hurt. Here was someone else whose death he could avenge.

"Don't look back," Reilly said. "You got a lot of life ahead of you. And from what I see between you and Roxanna, you don't want to throw away a future that could make you a happy man."

Ben swallowed hard and stared at the rough ceiling.

"I was twenty and a new deputy," Reilly said, "when my wife and baby died in childbirth. I thought my life was over. I could have remarried, except I just couldn't bring myself to go through that again. I knew other ladies after that. Some were mighty fine, but I couldn't take another chance. But now I'm pushing seventy, and I'm real sorry I didn't find someone to share my life. It pains me to think about it."

Ben listened with his eyes closed as Reilly continued.

"A man has to deal with a lot as he gets older and all the while, the years just keep on passing. And then it's too late. No matter what happens in a man's life, Ben, even if it's rotten and unfair, the trick is to keep getting older *and* wiser. Not just older."

Ben closed his eyes, knowing Reilly spoke the truth. After meeting Roxanna and her uncle, after facing Dejado, and now learning he had no real past love over which to brood, he knew his only option had to be the future. He'd wasted three years on a fantasy. He couldn't do it anymore.

A gust of wind rattled the shutters, and rain made music on the jailhouse roof. Weary from facing death and killing Dejado, and from the shocks of the evening, Ben finally fell asleep.

Long after midnight, Chandler Strong pounded on the door at the Kendall ranch house. Conchita, a robe about her, finally opened it.

He pushed her aside and strode in. Lamplight shone from the front room. "Where's Mrs. Kendall?"

"I'm here, Chandler," Vera said from the landing. She waved her hand. "Go back to bed, Conchita." She came the rest of the way down slowly, showing off how pretty she looked in her blue dressing gown, but he had something other than romance on his mind. He waited while Conchita started up the stairs, then followed Vera into the parlor.

Chandler lit the lamps, stoked the dwindling fire and added more wood, then sat on the settee facing the hearth. Something had stirred him up, Vera could tell. She sat by his side and rested her hand on his arm. "What's wrong?"

"Remember how you thought it would be a nice touch to have that actress wear your locket? To convince Ben you were dead?"

"Yes."

"Sara Hawks showed that locket to Roxanna at supper. The waiter came and told me."

Vera put her hand to her throat. "Oh, no."

"They know who you are."

Panic gripped her, and for a moment she couldn't speak. Then she found her voice. "What can we do?"

He frowned. "We'll have to move fast. When we're safe, you can mail Loophole power of attorney at his office down in Texas so he can sell the ranch. We'll contact him later on where to send the money."

"Won't he ask questions?"

"He won't know what's happening here or who we really are. He won't question your title because no one knows we're already married."

"Ten years next month," she said, squeezing his hand.

He lifted her hand to his lips and kissed her fingers.

"You trust Loophole?" she asked.

"Why not? You'll be his client. A nice, forlorn widow lady."

"But if he learns the truth about us?"

"No need for him to find out. We can do it all by mail, and he has no love for this place so he won't come up in person."

"But Brian, if he learns about the deed . . . ?"

"If he does, I'll make sure nobody can find us. The money could rot in the bank before I'd let them. Right now we have to move."

"I'll pack right away."

"Just take what you can put on the saddle." He kissed her on the cheek. "I'll get Frye, but we need traveling money."

"There's some in the safe here. Maybe three thousand."

"Not enough," he said. "We'll double back, hit the express office at Carmody."

She stared at him. "Brian, are you out of your mind?"

"Reilly's got to be heading out here come morning. That'll leave the town wide open. They'll never expect it. While they're halfway here, we'll be halfway to some real cash. We'll take a southern circle, miss 'em."

"But where could we go?"

"There's a hideout at Little Bend, a ghost town just across the border in Arizona Territory. We'll find a lot of our kind over there. While Hawks and his friends are on their way back to town, we'll be on our way to the border. Like ships passing in the night. Frye will bring some of our men with us. Katz and Hatcher can stake out fresh horses to pick up on our way back through the hills."

"But what if they track us down?"

He smiled. "I have an idea for some insurance."

It took her a moment to figure out what he meant. Then she shook her head. "I know what you're thinking, and you're wrong. You grab her, they'll never stop looking for us."

"Vera, they won't stop anyway," he said. "Most likely they'll think we went to Mexico. If it rains again, it'll wash out our tracks. They'll have no idea where we've gone. So what are you worried about?"

She shivered. "Brian, I can't face Ben Hawks."

"Why not? It was all a game with him, remember? Just another role for you to play. And you always were a great actress."

"He really fell for me."

Brian squeezed her hand. "So did I."

She turned to his embrace. Afraid to tell him she'd found herself falling for Ben and was glad to slip away from him, she kissed Brian with newly mustered passion.

A decent man like Ben could never be in her future. She had to be satisfied with men like Brian Avery and the devoted Harry Frye.

Deadly men.

As daylight spread across the rolling land, Ben, Hack, and Reilly headed west toward the Lazy K. Sloan and four armed, seasoned deputies brought up the rear. The rain ended, and the sun rose bright in a clearing sky.

All the way, Ben tried to deny the truth, but now it made a lot of sense. It felt like he'd been relieved of a terrible burden, a load he'd carried for three years. Yet if Vera Kendall was really

Lora, it didn't answer all the other questions haunting him now about her lies and what really happened on the Tucson stagecoach. Or why she was working with Avery.

He'd find out soon enough.

By the time they reached the Kendall ranch in the late afternoon, only the maid Conchita was at the house. There were no men in sight at the bunkhouse or corrals. Ben and Reilly remained mounted, alert for trouble, as Hack searched inside.

Ben sat restless in the saddle, afraid to see Vera Kendall face to face. Yet he knew facing the truth was the only way to be fully set free of the past.

Conchita came outside with Hack and stood on the porch. Her dark hair pinned back, an apron over her print dress, she looked worn down. Hack pushed his hat back and drew a deep breath. "She says Chandler Strong came by last night," Hack said. "Vera rode off with him and some others."

Ben grimaced as he leaned on the pommel of his saddle. Postponing the inevitable felt even more grueling. He wanted to see Vera and get it over and done.

Reilly looked around. "They could have headed for Mexico. Or Arizona Territory, but Mexico's more likely. Ain't no law of ours can follow 'em there."

Conchita brightened and held up her hand. "Señor Marshal, I hide last night and listen while they talk. She calls him Brian. She is a bad woman. He is her husband all this time. Ten years, she say."

"What?" Hack looked thunderstruck. Shock chilled Ben's heart, and he couldn't speak. The charade had been even more evil than he imagined. Lora was married when he'd proposed, wed to the very outlaw Ben had blamed for her death.

"She called him Brian?" Hack demanded. "Chandler Strong is Brian Avery?"

Conchita nodded. "He say they need money. They go back to Carmody."

"The express office," Reilly said with a frown. "What else did they say?"

Conchita shrugged. "I could not hear it all. He call her an actress. Then he say he has friends, some place called little something. In Arizona. I went to my room quick after that, because I was afraid."

Ben straightened in the saddle. He had steeled himself to see Vera, or Lora, or whoever she might be. Now he felt drained. The sweet woman he'd loved had been married to Brian Avery for ten years. An actress who spun her charm around Ben like a spider's web. He felt like a fool.

Reilly tipped his hat to Conchita. "Thanks." As Hack came off the porch and swung up in the saddle, the marshal eyed him and Ben. "Maybe we'll catch 'em on the way back to town."

Ben shook his head. "They're long gone by now. Even longer by the time we get to Carmody."

Reilly reined his horse around. "Then we'll make plans and go after 'em."

Conchita watched them ride away and made a decision. That fancy porcelain bathtub upstairs. The one she had to constantly fill with hot water for the demanding Vera. It needed another filling of hot water and bubbles, this time for Conchita, and no one could stop her.

She smiled and hurried back inside.

Ben, Reilly, and Hack, along with Sloan and the deputies, headed back to Carmody as fast as they could ride without killing their horses. It was midnight before they reached town. Sure enough, the express office had been robbed hours before, the clerk beaten to death.

After tending to their tired mounts, the posse gathered in the jailhouse by lamplight to make plans. "We'd better rest up, get a few more men, and hit the trail come sunup," Reilly said.

Hack nodded. "I already sent Buckley for help. You'll have as many more ranch hands as I can spare. You got authority in Arizona Territory?"

"I may be assigned here," Reilly said, "but I'm still a federal officer. I have authority anywhere the government does. And Avery'd be a feather in my cap."

He and Hack looked at Ben, who sat on the cot. His stillness worried Reilly.

"Ben, you go on back to the hotel," Hack said. "Send Buckley over here, and you get a good night's sleep. Make sure your ma and Roxanna stay put."

Ben nodded and got up, pulled his hat down tight, and reached for a slicker.

"We'll leave at daybreak," Reilly told him.

Sloan and the deputies took their cue and left to go bunk down at the stables. Hack let Ben outside in the rain and barred the door behind him.

"That's a nice boy," Reilly said.

Hack nodded and poured himself some strong coffee.

"You won't sleep good with that," Reilly said.

"I won't sleep anyway."

"I'm not sure it's good if Ben sees that woman," Reilly grunted.

"Only way he can put it behind him."

"I can lock her up for conspiracy and as an accessory, but it's Avery I really want."

"So does Ben."

Reilly nodded. "We have to get to Avery before he does."

"If we can."

★ ★ ★ ★ ★

In his room at the hotel, Ben lay staring at the ceiling with the lamp turned low, trying to account for the past three years, for the men he had killed. All for the wrong woman. Once they caught up with her and Avery, it would be over. His hunt, his vengeance trail, all behind him.

And then what?

How could a woman like Roxanna even consider a man who had been a gullible fool and so alone for so long? That dream had to be beyond his reach.

Finally, out of exhaustion, he slept.

Two hours before daylight, armed and ready to ride, a slicker over his arm, Ben left his hotel room. He lingered on the landing in the dim night-time lamplight, listening to the rain and wind rattle the windows and pound on the roof. It would be a long hard ride.

He turned away from the empty lobby below and walked down the hall, where he knocked on Sara's door. He had to let his mother know they were leaving. As he waited for her to answer, he reflected on what she'd given him all his life. Sara Hawks had always shared her strength and deep faith. She'd taught him to pray and believe, even in the face of the worst days. He'd lost some of that endurance on the vengeance trail, but he'd never lost faith. He needed that now to face up to the Kendall woman.

After a long while, his mother opened the door. Her dark hair spilled over the shoulders of her robe. When she saw him, Sara smiled. "Ben, when did you get back?"

"Around midnight."

"Did you see Vera?"

"No." He pushed his hat back. "But we found out she's an actress, been married to Brian Avery for ten years. He goes by the name of Chandler Strong around here."

"Oh, my."

"When we got to the ranch, they were gone. They must have passed us as we were heading out there. It looks like Avery hit the express office. They got in through the back. We think the clerk fell asleep at his desk. They forced him to open the safe, then killed him."

At his description, she paled. "I never heard anything."

"No one did. We'll pick up their trail come daylight."

"Oh, Ben, is it worth it now? If Lora never was, there's no reason for you to chase a bad woman and these men and get yourself killed."

"They murdered the stage driver, who had a wife and nine children. They killed the guard and other passengers and sacrificed an innocent young woman. And they killed a lot of men around here. They set Pecos and Dejado on me. And what's more, Reilly needs help. Hack and me, we'll be with him all the way."

"Ben, I have a bad feeling about this."

He half smiled. "Don't give me that Comanche dreaming again."

"I've always been right, haven't I?" she said. "And so were you when you told me you couldn't believe Lora had died, that you kept seeing her in your dreams."

Ben nodded. Maybe he did have his mother's gift.

"Do you want to talk to Roxanna?"

Reluctant, he shook his head. "She'll be sleeping."

"I doubt it. She's worried sick about you and her uncle."

"You go ahead. I have to leave."

"Ben Hawks, I know what you're thinking. Yes, you were tricked once, and that's a fact. But Roxanna's no ghost. She's for real, and she's worried about you."

"I get out of this, I'm going back to Texas."

"So you're through with women?"

"That's right."

She frowned. "That's a lot of foolish talk. And you know better."

"I've got to go."

"Sure, run away, but if ever I saw a man in love, it's you. And I don't mean with that phony actress. I'm talking about Roxanna."

"Ma, I'm all used up." He couldn't tell her how he felt about Roxanna. Not with what he still had to face, still had to risk.

"That's foolish talk, too."

He leaned in and kissed her cheek. "Pray for me."

Sara watched Ben walk away toward the landing. Her heart felt heavy, and she knew praying for him and the others was all she could do. He went on down the stairs, moving slowly as if already worn near to nothing. She kept watching until he was out of sight. Then she hurried to Roxanna's room and knocked softly.

The door opened by itself, just an inch or two. Sara hesitated. "Roxanna?"

Hearing no answer, she entered, fumbling for the lamp on the dresser by the door. Her hand closed on the matches. In the pale light from the hall, she could see the window curtains blowing.

"Roxanna?" She lit the lamp and turned up the flame.

Wild disarray and the open window greeted her. There was no sign of Roxanna. The girl's Winchester rifle lay at a slant against the night table, as if it had fallen there.

"Dear God, no!" Heart in her throat, her imagination caught up in fear, she could hardly breathe. Briefly as she'd known Roxanna, the girl had become like a daughter to her.

She ran out and down the hallway to the head of the stairs.

Down in the lobby, she saw Ben donning his slicker. "Ben," she called out. "Come here, quick."

CHAPTER TWENTY

At Sara's shout, Ben turned from struggling with his slicker to look up at her.

"Ben, she's gone! Roxanna's gone!"

Hit hard with new terror, Ben caught his breath. Then he bounded up the steps onto the landing and followed his mother to Roxanna's room.

Sara led the way inside. She turned the lamp higher, giving Ben a clear view of the devastation. Roxanna's blankets, cover, and pillow lay on the floor, jumbled together with a hairbrush and a fallen hand mirror, as if after a fierce struggle.

"Her riding clothes are gone," Sara said. "And her boots. She laid them out before going to bed. And her rifle . . ." Sara gestured toward the Winchester that leaned where it had fallen against the night table. "Like she tried to grab for it, but they got her first."

At the open window, curtains blew with the wind and rain. Ben stood frozen, his hand on his right holster, staring at the empty bed. No pain could match what he felt as he realized how very much he loved that fiery young woman. How much he wanted to be with her, laugh with her, hold her in his arms. Live his life with her.

"Ben, are you listening? They took Roxanna. Her window opens onto the veranda. And there's a back stairway."

Ben shivered down to his boots. "She's a hostage, to keep us at bay."

"And when they don't need her anymore?"

He couldn't think about that. "I've got to tell Hack and Reilly."

She caught his arm. "Son, be careful."

He bent and kissed her cheek, then headed out. He rushed to the stairs and down, taking them three steps at a time, then moving through the dim lobby and outside into the dark street where rain fell. His heart beat so fast, he feared it would jump up his throat. He ran across the muddy street, praying under his breath. "Dear God, please, protect her."

At the jail, rain dripping from his hat brim, he banged on the door and charged inside to tell a stunned Hack and the marshal what had happened. Then, his knees like water, he sat down at the table across from them as they stared at him in a long, painful silence.

Hack looked shattered at the thought of his niece in the hands of those men. Reilly pulled himself together and poured Ben a cup of hot coffee. "Ben, you need to eat something," he said.

Ben shook his head and drank the harsh brew as fast as possible. Cold and numb, he could hardly feel the chair beneath him. "She's a hostage," he muttered.

Hack abruptly gulped his own coffee down. Ben saw the fear he felt for Roxanna in Hack's and Reilly's faces. Avery's ruthless outlaws would probably fight over her. She'd get no help from Vera and most likely none from Avery.

"We don't know how many men they've got," Reilly said at length. "Signs in back of the express office showed maybe five or six horses, but they're sure to tie up with more."

"I'm not waiting for sunup," Hack said. "The rain's gonna wash out their tracks." He tugged at his hat brim. "Conchita said they said they were going to 'little' something in Arizona Territory. Crossing over those mountains is tough; they're pretty high and rugged. Avery's gang might head south to the stage road for easy riding."

Reilly frowned and shook his head. "I've been thinking. I'll bet it's Little Bend, that old ghost town right across the Arizona border, maybe a couple days from here. It's a hard ride, but it's due west."

Ben got to his feet and downed the rest of his coffee. "Let's go."

Hack pulled on his coat. "Listen to that rain. It'll be daylight soon."

"I might be wrong," Reilly said. "Look, you and Ben head due west for the border. I'll take some deputies and circle the area for signs in case they headed some other direction, and if not, we'll catch up with you."

"I'll send Sloan and the boys to the Kendall ranch first," Hack said. "If they didn't go that way, my people can still meet up with us. And I'll have 'em bring spare horses."

Reilly agreed. "All right. I've already arranged for food and water for a week."

Ben paced, willing to let the older men take charge. At least until he could control his burning anxiety.

Hack and Ben, both wearing slickers, saddled their horses in the livery stables. The other riders had left moments before.

"Sorry about this," Ben said.

Hack's voice rasped. "Not your fault."

"If I hadn't come here, Avery and that woman wouldn't have panicked. They wouldn't have taken Roxanna."

"Ben, you were doing what you had to do."

Ben shook his head and readied his mount.

Sara came inside out of the rain, a slicker over her head. She hugged and kissed her son. "Get back to the hotel, Ma," he said, a blush rising in his cheeks.

"We have to go," Hack told her. He quickly turned to tighten the cinch and drop the stirrup. She moved to his side and laid a hand on his arm.

"Don't you worry," she said, gazing up at Hack when he turned toward her. "Your niece is so ornery, they'll be glad to give her back."

Hack gazed down at Sara. He saw something shining in her eyes. He dared not think it was interest. Yet her touch put him in a dither. Moments from riding off into mortal danger, it was an odd thing to be thinking. Then again, maybe not.

Sara reached a soft hand up to Hack's neck, pulled his head down, and kissed him square on the mouth. Hack's knees buckled. As she drew back, he could still taste the woman of her. "Come back alive, Hack Larabee."

"Yes, ma'am."

She shook her head and smiled. "You haven't got it straight yet, have you?"

Embarrassed but dancing on air, Hack tipped his hat. He turned to his bay and mounted. A woman like Sara wouldn't kiss just any man, especially on the lips, and he felt like he'd been chosen. Except for his worry over Roxanna, his heart would have been singing.

Ben swung into the saddle as his mother blew him a kiss. He and Hack rode out of the livery and headed west, hunched over in the rain and rising wind as daylight came.

Neither spoke about Sara's giving Hack such a loving kiss. Yet it wouldn't leave Hack's mind or heart.

After a time, Ben said, "If they came this way, they sure didn't leave any tracks."

"It's been raining pretty hard," Hack said.

Before long they reached high, rugged territory, fighting through rocks and brush, dodging pinyon pines. Once they saw deer sheltering, and bear tracks on a slope the rain had missed.

Riding due west would be a shortcut, even though it felt impossible with the rocky terrain, rampant undergrowth, and thick junipers often in their path.

They kept going, ignoring the rain as best they could. After a while, Hack gave Ben a warning glance. "Watch out for flash floods."

Ben nodded and kept his eyes peeled.

They rode most of the day, their mounts dragging under the strain. For a time they followed a rushing creek and things felt easier, but they were soon back in unforgiving terrain. The heavy downpour slowed them often. Lagging behind Hack, Ben prayed softly for the Lord's help. He figured Hack was praying the same. Would that help the Lord hear them? Was God even paying attention?

When night fell, they made camp beneath overhanging boulders, even as the rain noisily pounded the rocks around them. They ate jerky and hardtack next to a sheltered fire that barely burned the piled brush and recovered dung.

"We'll leave early," Hack said. "Try to make better time. And hope Reilly and the others catch up with us before we get there."

He said not a word about Roxanna's safety. Ben understood why. He couldn't bring himself to even say her name. He stared into their tiny fire, brooding over the last three wasted years of his life. Lora Bedloe was a conniving woman who'd led him down the garden path. He'd suffered for her, killed for her. And now Roxanna might die, because of the deceiver he'd thought he loved.

"When it all comes down to it," Hack said at length, "the only thing that matters is getting Roxanna out alive. And you know, Ben, I've been thinking what a miserable old man I've gotten to be."

"Old man? You're not even sixty."

"Fifty-five next month. But I got to remembering how it was, holding my wife in my arms while I slept. A man can't find a better peace than that."

Ben had no answer, fearful such a blessing might never be his to enjoy.

They fell silent awhile. Then Hack continued. "You have to know, I'm leading up to something. I could be mighty happy with a feisty woman like your ma. When she kissed me, I got to tell you, I plumb fell apart."

"She gave you a sign, all right."

"You wouldn't stop me?"

"Who, me?" Ben shook his head. "I'd say you'll have your hands full, and if you got her to say yes, well, your life would never be the same."

"I can see that. Of course, maybe I'm wrong about her being interested."

"She's interested. It was your room at the hotel and no one else's she wanted to confiscate."

Hack smiled and then sobered. Ben stared at the crackling fire. He had no answers. He prayed silently for Roxanna's safety, for a chance to let her know she could walk all over him if she so chose. To bare what he began to realize minutes after Roxanna had been stolen. That he loved Roxanna and only her.

CHAPTER TWENTY-ONE

Late the next day, Roxanna and her captors arrived at the shabby remains of Little Bend, a ghost town that had died with failure at the diggings. The few men posted as lookouts recognized Avery and let the riders through. With a sinking heart, Roxanna guessed the heavy downpour would keep Ben and anyone else from following them, or even knowing which way the outlaws had gone.

Some of the men took the horses to the old livery barn east of town. Avery and the others, with Roxanna firmly in tow, settled in the saloon where another thirty outlaws caroused at gambling tables run by those wanted men who had chosen to live there. Many hung out at the bar. The wood floor stank of spilled whiskey. Smoke hung in the air. Lamplight flickered on ugly faces. The only heat came from an iron stove near the bar.

Roxanna sat huddled against the west wall of the saloon, her hair unkempt around her face. The blanket Avery had tossed her for warmth did little against the chill of her wet clothes. Her dark eyes scanned the smoky, crowded room, watching the outlaws' every move. So many ugly, wretched men, each casting slimy glances her way.

She prayed softly to survive, to be rescued or escape. Terror of some vile man putting his hands on her made her regret all the more what she had not told Ben Hawks—that she loved him, honored and trusted him. That she wanted to spend her life with him. She hadn't fully realized it until the gunfight with

Dejado, when Ben so easily could have died. Now it could be too late. She had to find a way to escape. How? Running for the door would be foolish. She'd be stopped in seconds.

She looked around the room. To her left stood an empty chair, while to her right Vera Kendall sat with an empty glass. Pretty as she was, Vera looked fiercer and wilder than Roxanna could have imagined. Vera smelled of whiskey and old rose perfume. On Vera's other side, Frye sat with a glass of rye and a half-empty bottle on the table in front of him.

Vera reached for his glass and drank from it. Then she took Frye's rolled smoke and puffed on it. He scowled at her.

"Brian catches you," Frye said, "he'll blame me."

Vera smiled and returned the hand-rolled smoke to him. "I can handle Brian. Where is he, anyhow?"

"Getting rooms."

"He should sell this woman and get it over with."

Roxanna glared at her. "You apparently have been sold three or four times."

Vera sneered. Tipsy at least, Roxanna guessed. "Darling, you are in no position to be catty."

"First you act like an angel to fool a nice man like Ben Hawks," Roxanna said, "and you get a lot of people killed. And then you marry the Kendall ranch and get both brothers shot dead. And all this time, even with Ben, you were already married to a murderous outlaw."

Frye grunted. "Vera was always a great actress."

Vera reached for the bottle and filled her own glass. She smiled at Frye's displeasure.

Roxanna, simmering with deep anger, studied the woman. "You look a lot older than Ben."

"Yes," Frye said, sounding amused. "When the war ended, she was twenty, so that makes her, let's see, thirty-four."

Vera made a face that twisted her mouth. Despite Roxanna's

fears, she couldn't help enjoying the woman's sudden anger. "You can both sit there and say whatever you like, but Miss Larabee is going to belong to one of those ugly men before we leave town."

"Unless something happens to Brian," Frye said. He nodded toward the staircase on one side of the saloon. Avery was coming down, no longer Chandler Strong, but still a dandy, freshly dressed in a white shirt and red vest with his diamond stickpin. He walked over to the roulette table, joining Posher and Pinkley. They were scowling, and Roxanna figured the house didn't pay much.

"Look at him, Harry," Vera said. "Brian's indestructible."

Roxanna drew her blanket more tightly about her. "I'm wondering just how Laird Kendall really died. Who shot him in the back?"

Vera fussed with her hair. "Rossiter."

Roxanna couldn't grasp that. "But he was also . . ."

"Shot down?" Vera said with a smirk. "We used him and then got rid of him because he was drinking and gambling too much, and Brian was afraid he'd shoot off his mouth."

"Vera, you talk too much," Frye said.

"And who shot Miles?" Roxanna wanted to know.

"Oh, Brian hired them out of Texas," Vera said.

"Wonderful," Roxanna muttered.

Vera snickered. "If you must know, Brian was calling the shots the whole time. He was only courting you to get your ranch. He certainly wasn't interested in a simpering thing like you when he already had me. No, my dear, he could care less about you, and that's why he's going to sell you."

"Vera, let it go," Frye said.

She pursed her lips. "I know what I'm saying. She'll never leave this town alive."

"Brian's a little fonder of her than you think. When he leaves again, he may just take her along."

"Not if I have anything to say about it." Vera downed her drink and got up from behind the table, pushing her way around Roxanna. She stumbled, then moved through the all-too-friendly crowd to join Brian. Roxanna stared after her, trying to stifle her panic.

Frye slid over next to Roxanna. "You have a choice," he said. "Hook up with me and you'll be safe, or you can hope Brian doesn't sell you to one of those men that keep watching you."

Defiant, she lifted her chin. "My uncle and Ben, and the marshal, they'll find me."

"When do you think that will be? And why would they even come this far out of the way? No one knows about this place. And the rain washed out our tracks."

"If you're trying to scare me," she said, "it's working."

"Just making an offer."

"And who would save me from you?"

"You don't have many options," he said. "And the worst of those men watching you like you're chocolate candy are not members of Avery's gang. There'd be no rules. No one to help you."

She could see he had no real interest in her. Apparently he still had some tiny spark of decency, but she couldn't count on it. She shivered under her blanket as two big men turned from a nearby poker table, leaned back in their chairs, and studied her with interest and stifled passion.

"Some are ruthless," Frye said, "and all are on the dodge. Some for murder. Except for Vera, there are no other women in this forsaken place. There'd be a big fight over you if they weren't so afraid of Brian Avery. They'll have to pay to get past him."

"What can I do?"

"Like I said. Be nice to me."

She gazed at him a long moment, then looked away. "I don't understand you, Mr. Frye. You seem to be a well-educated man. How did you get mixed up with Brian Avery and that woman?"

He poured himself more whiskey—his third at least—and leaned closer. "I was a lawyer and just starting out when Vera came along, but she only wanted someone with money, like Avery. I fell for her so hard I ended up riding with him and his partisans in the war. Because of her."

The man must be drunk, to be so confiding. Either that, or he was sure she'd never get a chance to tell any of this to anyone. "Why did you stay with him after it was all over?"

"I'd lost my fitness for practicing law or any other decent job. And there was no denying he was making us all rich."

"Like with that stage robbery?"

He didn't even ask which robbery she referred to. "That was the big one, all right."

A fistfight broke out near the bar. Two big men, too intoxicated to hit each other with their wild swings, finally collapsed on stools and went back to guzzling rye. The brief excitement over, Roxanna turned to Frye. "Ben never saw through her."

"Like I said, Vera was a great actress. Had glowing reviews when she was on the stage. When Brian heard about some bonanza shipment being planned, he had her change her name, make herself look innocent, and go shine up to Ben Hawks. Being a Texas Ranger and well known, he could help her get the job at the express company. It all happened pretty fast." He paused to pour more whiskey in his glass. "When time came for the shipment, she lied about having a cousin in California, just to get a pass. She had this actress friend who wanted to get to California but had no money. Vera let her take the pass and told her to pretend she was Vera so she could use it."

"In the locket, Vera had dark hair."

"It was a wig," Frye said.

191

"And Ben couldn't tell the difference?"

He chuckled at that. "Honey, men are foolish around a beautiful woman." He sipped his drink. "So later on, when she came to Carmody, the plan was to zero in on Laird Kendall, then take over both the Kendall and the Larabee ranch."

Roxanna raised an eyebrow. "So Chandler, I mean Brian, courting me was part of it."

Frye nodded and stared across the crowded room at Vera and Avery. The two of them stood close together, laughing, Avery's arm around Vera's shoulders as the roulette wheel spun.

"And all this time, he and Vera were married," Roxanna said.

Frye's tone was bitter, the yearning in his face for Vera all too clear. "Brian used everyone, including her."

Roxanna shivered at the horror of it. She recalled what Reilly had said when they first realized Lora Bedloe was Vera Kendall, about the plotters needing to keep the dead woman's identity a secret. Could she get Frye to admit what they'd planned? "One thing I don't understand. Why didn't anyone see it wasn't really Lora Bedloe who died in the robbery?"

For a moment, Frye wore a haunted expression. "The plan was to ruin her looks. Turned out they didn't have to. When we got down to the wreck, they were all dead. When the stagecoach crashed, she got hit in the face. So the secret was safe enough."

"My God." It took a long while for Roxanna to shake that awful thought from her mind.

"Avery's men," she asked at length, "do they stay with him just for the money?"

"They rode with us in Kansas and were loyal to him because he was a good leader, which I hate to admit. He also made sure they never rotted in jail. They accepted that if they couldn't be rescued, they'd be killed before they could talk. I think they liked it that the rules were the same for all of them, including Avery. Plus, they always got a good share of the money. They could come and go as they pleased without reparation."

Roxanna paused, watching Vera hanging on to Avery as he gambled. "Why did Avery go partisan instead of joining the regular army?"

"Flunked out of West Point," Frye said with great satisfaction. "Also, it was too important to him to be a big shot, be the boss with a free hand."

Again that bitterness in his voice. He had to be a disappointed man. He'd lost his profession and turned outlaw for a woman he would never have. She could almost admire how he'd given up so much for so little and yet still loved Vera.

He was jealous of Avery, that much was clear. Maybe she could use that. She looked around the noisy room, smelled the smoke and liquor. "You don't belong with these men. You're better than Avery and the rest." She leaned closer to him. "Will you help me get away?" she whispered.

Frye shook his head. "No, because he'd string me up for it. He once hanged one of his own men, real slow, in front of us."

Horrified, she stared at Frye. "Why?"

"The man stabbed his bunk mate to death."

Roxanna leaned back and shivered. "What about that man Brownie they took to Mesilla? If he gets scared and talks . . ."

Frye shrugged. "I heard he's been busted out and is on his way to Mexico."

He fell silent as Brian and Vera came over to their table. Vera looked annoyed and restless. Brian Avery tipped his hat to Roxanna. He held a cigar, and his pale eyes glistened in the lamplight. She could read his feelings for her in them, and it gave her hope.

"We have rooms upstairs," Brian said. "Vera's going to stay with you, Miss Roxanna, just for safekeeping."

"Why do you need me?" Roxanna asked. She'd already guessed the answer, but she wanted to hear him say it.

He pulled out a chair. "Just in case they track us down."

Before Brian or Vera could sit, a pair of husky men with thick mustaches and dirty shirts came over. They both smelled of sweat and looked mean as rabid dogs. One of them, a couple of inches taller than the other, looked at Roxanna as if stripping her not only of her blanket but the clothing beneath. "Hey, Avery, what do you want for the darker-haired one?"

Avery chuckled. "Ask me in the morning. I may want to travel light."

"Well, remember we was here first. Winter's coming, and nights get plenty cold."

The men leered hungrily at Roxanna and turned away.

Vera made a face. "Why don't you sell her now, Brian? Then I could be with you tonight, instead of having to watch her."

Avery looked from Vera to Roxanna. The indecision in his face turned Vera's cheeks an angry red beneath the powder she wore. "I'm your wife," she reminded him. "For ten years now."

He reached out to stroke her jawline. "You worry too much."

She pouted. "Do we have to stay in this filthy place?"

He looked around. "Until the weather clears."

"Then California?"

He nodded. "Like I promised."

Vera cast a sneer at Roxanna, letting her know *she'd* never see California. Avery met Roxanna's eyes again, and this time she saw regret there—not much, no more than a man might have at passing up an extra slice of cake.

The smoke, noise, and smell of whiskey made Roxanna feel ill. She shuddered under her blanket as Avery turned away.

Vera glared at Roxanna. "You stay put." Swiftly, she crossed the room in Avery's wake.

Frye watched Vera go, misery so clear in his face that Roxanna felt sorry for him. "Why do you stay around and suffer?"

Frye shook his head. "I can't help it. Maybe someone will

back shoot him and I can step in."

"Not face on?"

He set about rolling another smoke. "He's too fast," he said.

"Faster than Ben Hawks?"

"Maybe."

"I know Ben's looking for me," she said. "With a posse."

"But they won't find this place. Like I told you, be nice to me and I'll keep you safe. Otherwise . . ." He trailed off, leaving the threat unspoken.

He didn't need to say it again. She knew exactly what he meant.

Late that night, the saloon had grown mostly quiet. The fights had stopped, though gambling continued and liquor still flowed. Outside, noisy wind and rain persisted.

Upstairs in a dirty room, Vera and Roxanna stayed dressed in the chill and from fear of the bedding. The wooden walls had never been painted, and the floor swayed down in spots. An oil lamp burned low on the dresser.

Roxanna lay on top of the blankets on one of the two iron-frame beds. The mattress rocked on ropes and slats under her. She kept her coat over her, preferring it to the blankets that might contain Lord-only-knows what vermin.

Vera had locked the door from the inside. She slipped the key under her pillow and hiccupped, then sneered at Roxanna. "Don't bother stealing it," Vera warned. "You walk out on that landing, there's no place to go."

Roxanna knew that. The landing only led to the crowded saloon below. If she went that way, she'd lose Avery's protection in a split second. The men would be all over her.

She lay quiet, hoping Vera would go to sleep first.

Rain beat at the shutters on the single window between the two beds. Dirty curtains dangled in front of it and rustled as wind found its way inside through the warped frame. As Roxanna stared at the window, an idea slowly took shape. It could be her only hope.

Vera, clearly intoxicated, reclined on her bed. "Brian's going to sell you first thing in the morning."

The prospect terrified her, though she fought not to let this woman see it. "Let me get away, Vera."

Vera laughed. "Forget it."

"You saw the way he looked at me. I'll do anything to survive, and then you'll be out."

Vera snickered. "Brian would never want a pansy like you."

Nerves already raw, Roxanna's temper got the better of her. "Were you born this way, Vera? Nasty and selfish and so greedy you don't care who dies or gets hurt, so long as you get what you want?"

"You listen to me." Sounding dazed with drink, Vera adjusted her pillow. "I grew up in the lap of luxury, and then my foolish father got us in debt, and we lost everything when I was eighteen. I was sore ashamed, but I learned how to get money, even went on the stage where everyone loved me. I was a great actress."

"I know. Everyone says so." Repairing the damage of moments before, Roxanna did her best to sound admiring. "But that's all the more reason you don't need me here."

"You have no say about anything. And I promise you, nothing is going to stand in my way, especially you. I don't care if Brian sells you or buries you, just so you're gone. So get some sleep. If you can."

Roxanna lay quiet again, listening to the rain. The lamp burned even lower. Before long, in the dim light it cast, she saw Vera breathing slowly as if falling asleep. She waited, listening to the small noises Vera made. An hour before daylight, when she thought Vera slept soundly, she got up and tried the window—

cautiously at first, praying it wouldn't stick or creak. Luck was with her. It slid up easily, and she opened the shutters.

The sudden noise of rain and wind awakened Vera. She sat up, rubbing her eyes. "Hey!"

Roxanna spun around. As Vera scrambled out of bed and reached for her, Roxanna slammed her fist into Vera's jaw, snapping her head back and knocking her flat on the bed. Vera lay there unconscious, arms flung out at her sides.

Roxanna's hand hurt. She shook it to ease the pain, then hurriedly donned her heavy coat and hat. What next? A blanket. She yanked one off of her own bed and tied it to the bedpost, then pulled it tight and eyed the length. About six feet, at a guess. It'd have to be enough. She bunched the woolly fabric in her arms and shoved it out the window, watching the far end fall in the rain.

She hoisted herself on the window sill and swung her legs over until they dangled against the outside wall. Rain blew against her. She would have given anything for her rifle or a revolver. As it was, she had to take a chance. She faced a long drop to the muddy ground with nothing to break her fall, but she remembered what she'd learned riding horses—if you were going to be bucked off, you should act like a drunken sailor and roll up like a ball. If she could shimmy down to the end of the blanket, she ought to survive the remaining distance. She hoped.

She took a deep breath, grabbed the blanket, and fell out into the black rain.

She hit the mud hard, knocking the breath out of her. She lay there a long moment, assessing her condition. Nothing hurt as bad as a broken bone, so she guessed she was all right. Suddenly, the back door of the saloon opened some twenty feet away. She sat up, hunched low in the downpour.

A big, bearded man in a grubby shirt appeared in the gap. Someone inside yelled, "Hey, Shanks! You're buying this round!"

Laughter followed as the man named Shanks leaned his rifle against the wall, just inside the doorway, and ambled out into the rain, his boots splashing in the puddles. He headed for the distant outhouse, finding his way in the lamplight that spilled from the saloon.

Roxanna stayed low and so still, she could hear her heart racing. Shanks was in a hurry, the rain beating on him as he reached the outhouse. He disappeared inside, yanking the warped door closed against the storm.

Roxanna got to her feet. Sliding around on the mud, she made it to the back door. When she peered down the hallway that led to the saloon proper, she saw the backs of two men at a table. The noise of other men rumbled, carrying back to her along with smoke and the stench of whiskey.

Shanks' rifle was a Winchester, same as her own. Quickly, she grabbed the gun and partially closed the saloon door. Busy in the outhouse, Shanks would know someone had stolen his rifle when he came back out, but hopefully, he'd figure it was someone inside. Or maybe he was already so drunk, he'd forget he'd taken it this far. She could only pray it would be hours before Vera came to and sounded the alarm.

She headed around the rear of the shacks in the downpour, hoping she could find that winding trail east. She had no light to guide her, only prayers and instinct. Knowing the horses had been left in the old livery barn behind the shacks at the east end of town, she moved that way as fast as she could. Her boots slid in the mud, and once she crashed up hard against a back wall. Drenched, she paused to take a deep breath in the dark storm, then kept going. She knew she had little time.

A horse's whinny let her know she'd reached the place she sought. To her surprise, she made out the dim shape of a mare standing under a lean-to against the south wall of the barn. Maybe it was lame or in foal, or in heat and causing problems.

Roxanna spoke softly to it as she moved inside the narrow space. The mare wore a halter, and it nosed her as she ran a hand over its neck and shoulder. Then she felt its legs. They were smooth and sturdy under her fingers, no sign of anything wrong.

There wasn't time to hunt through the dark barn for a saddle, and if she put Shanks' Winchester down, there was no guarantee she'd find it again. She'd ride bareback. "Sorry, old girl," she whispered, "but we're getting out of here."

She felt stiff and cold as she led the mare into the rain, moving as fast as she could. Winchester in one hand and halter in the other, she continued toward the darker shapes of some rocks where she could more easily mount.

A fist closed on her hair, jerking her backward. She gasped in horror and looked up at Shanks' ugly face.

CHAPTER TWENTY-TWO

Long before daybreak as the rain stopped, Ben and Hack rode the rough mountain trails, heading west toward Little Bend. They passed through dark pinyon pines and around massive boulders. At dawn, the storm gave way to a clearing sky. The rising light picked out little white flowers amid the brush and loose rock that made the going hard.

They came over a rise and saw distant buildings lined up near a wagon road. High terrain rose along both sides of the trail and the town. Only one building, at the far west end, had lights in the windows.

As they reined in under the trees, Hack spoke under his breath. "Looks like a saloon."

"I can see lots of horses in the barn. We're outnumbered."

"We can't wait," Hack said. "You take the back door."

Ben nodded agreement as they shed their slickers. "They've likely posted sentries," he said. "We take 'em quiet, and alive if we can."

They circled east of the town and reached the south side behind the shacks. A single gunman on guard duty lounged against a wall, sleepy-eyed. He barely had time to glance up when Ben's fist met his chin. The man toppled to the dirt, out cold. Hack tied him with his own gun belt, gagged him, then confiscated the six-guns. He tossed them into a water trough as they passed a dilapidated horse barn and headed west. A second sentry, dozing, posed no trouble at all.

A few minutes later they reached the rear of the saloon. Crammed full with smoke and noise and squabbling, it had a second story with windows all around. Ben glanced up, but saw nobody at any of them. Smoke came from a rock chimney at the west end of the building. Someone must be cooking breakfast.

Leaving their horses in an alley between the saloon and the next building to the east, Ben and Hack checked their weapons. Glancing around, Ben spotted the outhouse in the trees some distance away. Meanwhile, Hack headed through the alley toward the front of the saloon.

Slowly, Winchester in hand and twin six-guns ready, Ben opened the rear door and peered into a long hallway. Noise and smoke filled the main room beyond. A fellow's loud voice echoed, followed by laughter and catcalls. Ben moved into the hallway and flattened himself against the wall. Slowly, he inched as close as he dared to the saloon until he had a good view of the room. Everyone inside had their backs to him. A few empty plates sat on tables next to coffee cups. The smell of burned bread and old coffee cycled from a back room at the other side of the bar.

Someone shifted a few steps, allowing Ben a clearer view. In the center of the saloon floor, a big untidy man growled in fury at someone Ben couldn't see. "She's mine," the big man said. "I caught her."

"Back off, Shanks." The stern voice brought silence to the saloon and froze Ben where he stood. *Chandler Strong. Brian Avery.* He tightened his grip on his rifle. If Avery was here, then Roxanna was too. Where?

He ventured out a little further. Rough-looking men made a ragged half circle around Shanks, while others sat at a few tables. There were no women in view except Roxanna, held tight under Brian Avery's left arm. Ben's jaw clenched.

Avery held up Shanks' rifle with his right hand, then tossed the gun to the big man.

"I found her," Shanks said again. "She's mine."

"When I'm ready," Avery said. "She goes to the highest bidder."

"I ain't waiting," Shanks snarled. Heavy with liquor and passion and too much brass, he spread his feet and pushed his hat back. A holster hung crooked at his hip.

"You may be right." Avery threw Roxanna on the floor in a heap. She started crawling toward the front door. Harry Frye came quickly from a side table, grabbed Roxanna by the arm, and pulled her to her feet, moving back against the wall, his arm around her waist as if to hold her safe. He whispered something in her ear that Ben didn't catch, and she went still.

"You wouldn't let me ride with you," Shanks said to Avery.

"I never trusted you," Avery replied. "You were an army deserter."

"So what?"

Motion to his left, on the staircase beyond the bar, caught Ben's eye. A woman was coming down, in riding clothes with a blanket over her shoulders, her blonde hair ruffled. Ben caught his breath. It was Lora, or Vera, or whoever she was. His heart shriveled up and crumbled inside his chest.

He looked away from her and forced himself to concentrate on the nasty crowd in the saloon.

Shanks stood weaving, making a show of getting ready to draw.

Avery just smiled.

Ben had hunted this man for three years. Not just for the woman on the stairs, or at least who he thought she'd been, but for the many dead on that stagecoach. And for the dead in other robberies Avery had committed throughout the west. He realized the shadow of vengeance had been just that, a shadow.

Justice was his real target, and he felt better for it. But now what? Shoot Avery dead and bring every outlaw in the saloon after him? Let Shanks kill Avery, if he could, or watch Avery murder the big unkempt gunslinger in cold blood?

"Hey, Shanks," someone called. "You can't take Brian Avery. You're loco."

Shanks hesitated. Then he let his hands fall loose at his sides and turned away. "I'm too drunk anyway," the big man mumbled.

Avery turned toward Roxanna. The terror in her face ripped Ben like a knife. In that moment, he forgot everything and everyone, except her.

Avery dug his fingers in Roxanna's flowing hair, yanking her away from Frye.

Ben wasn't aware of moving out of the hallway and into the light, but he found himself standing in open space, the hard cases in the saloon all staring at him. He set his back to the wall near the bar, his rifle aimed from the hip at Avery.

"Who the devil is that?" Shanks muttered.

"Well, well. Ben Hawks," Avery said.

Shanks backed into the crowd. "Hawks? He killed Dejado. I ain't tangling with him."

The hostility in the room defused at the revelation, and the crowd of toughs backed off. Ben guessed why, and could have laughed at the irony of it. He was the former ranger who rode the starry sky. No one could kill him. Dime novels praised him as indestructible.

Alone among his outlaws, Brian Avery appeared undaunted. He let go of Roxanna. Frye swiftly stepped forward and dragged her back to the wall. Ben had to fight to keep from looking at the stairway where Vera stood, some twenty feet ahead of him. He kept his attention on Avery.

Avery spread his boots. "As Chandler Strong, I had to be

nice to you, Hawks. But we're in my town now, and I call the shots here."

Ben pitched his voice to carry. "I came for Miss Larabee."

"She's not going anywhere."

"And I'm taking you in for your murdering raids. For the murders on the Tucson stage back in '76. And for the express agent in Carmody."

Avery smiled. "You're standing here surrounded by my friends, in a hideout in the middle of nowhere, and you have the audacity to think you're leaving here alive?"

Ben swallowed, his mouth so dry it hurt. He'd become a brazen Texas Ranger all over again. His face burned. Where the devil was Hack? Somewhere outside the saloon's swinging front doors, unless he'd run afoul of another sentry they'd missed. No time to worry about that, only to deal with the situation in front of him. A good offense just might work.

"You took Dejado," Avery said with a sneer, "but I can take you, Hawks, right here and now, because I taught Dejado all he knew. And I saw you draw, remember? I hope I don't kill you dead. I've always wanted to hang a ranger, ain't that right, boys?"

A few onlookers nodded. Most merely watched, clearly still in awe of Ben Hawks and his reputation.

Roxanna squirmed in Frye's hold. Avery spoke again. "Tell you what, Hawks. You make this a fair fight and you win, you can ride out with Roxanna and no one here will stop you."

Ben figured no one in the room would keep that promise. But what choice did he have? Any chance to save Roxanna was worth the risk. He lowered his rifle, letting it rest on the floor, His right hand near his holster, he waited. He wanted Avery alive, but he had to keep Roxanna safe. A fair fight might keep the other men out of it until help arrived. Hack, or Reilly and his posse, or both.

Avery reached his left hand up as if to push his hat back. His eyes narrowed, and he suddenly drew with his right.

A split second faster, Ben's right hand whipped up his Colt like a flash of lightning. His shot rang out before Avery pulled the trigger.

The bullet hit Avery square between the eyes. The man staggered backward, chin in the air, then crashed to the floor and rolled on his side. Avery's shot seared across the left side of Ben's head. Stunned, he rocked sideways with the impact. From the staircase, he heard Vera Kendall scream.

In shock but his vision clear, he didn't feel any pain, though blood was running down his face toward his shoulder. He drew his left-hand Colt. The crowd gasped and drew back even further.

Frye pulled his six-gun, his left arm around Roxanna's waist, holding her in front of him, her back to his chest. "Drop it, Hawks."

Dazed, Ben hesitated.

Roxanna twisted around and punched Frye hard in the nose. Frye yelped in pain and fell against the wall as he shoved her violently to the floor.

The saloon's front doors flew open. Frye spun around as Hack fired from the doorway, hitting Frye in his gun arm and knocking him sideways. Frye dropped his weapon and gasped, grabbing his wound with his other hand. At the same moment, Posher and Pinkley emerged from the crowd and pulled their six-guns. From the swinging doors, Hack shot Posher before he could fire. Ben spun and got Pinkley, shooting him dead center. Both outlaws slammed back against the bar, then keeled over and fell flat. Blood began to pool around their fallen bodies.

The echo of the gunfire rang in the sudden hush.

Hack entered the saloon, rifle in his left hand, six-gun in his right. Roxanna got to her feet and hurried to her uncle.

Ben glanced at the stairway. Vera had turned and started back up.

A murmur ran through the rest of the hard men in the saloon. As Ben listened, calculating the mood and their chances of getting out alive, he heard a rough, wonderful voice behind him. "Step aside, Ben," Reilly said from the back entrance.

Behind Hack at the front, Sloan and two deputies walked up. Four Larabee hands appeared just inside the swinging doors.

Ben turned. Behind Reilly, he saw two more deputies.

The toughs in the saloon withdrew into huddles. "Drop your gun belts," Reilly said as he and his deputies advanced into the room. "And I mean now."

The toughs obeyed, each one of them putting his hands up.

With Roxanna safe at her uncle's side, Ben turned toward the staircase, his heart throbbing like crazy, his head wound painful and bleeding as he holstered his six-guns. He had one more thing to do before he could go to Roxanna.

Up the steps he went, two at a time. He caught up to Vera at the door of her room, grabbed her wrist, and spun her to face him. Touching her revolted him, and he threw her against the wall.

She barely managed to stay upright. Seeing her now—a stranger, her hair blonde instead of dark, her face powdered, a large purpling bruise on her chin and her pale brown eyes filling with fake tears—he felt the past drain away even as she moved toward him. "Oh, Ben, I'm so glad it's over. You don't know what it was like, being taken prisoner by those men."

He stepped away from her. "You were married to Avery when we met."

"It's not true."

"We'll see what Harry Frye has to say about it."

"He'll lie."

"*You* lied, three years ago. You used me to get that job. You set up the robbery, and you were there when the driver and guard and passengers were killed. That makes you a co-conspirator and an accessory to grand larceny and murder. And we haven't even gotten around to Laird Kendall. Or Miles."

The false tears spilled over. "Oh, Ben, please let me go. If you ever loved me, you must."

"I don't know you. I never did."

She put her hand to her throat. "What are you going to do?"

"You and Frye will stand trial."

Briefly, her voice hardened. "You'll never prove anything."

"One of you will make a deal."

"Please, you know you still love me."

Sick to his gut, Ben gestured. "Just get down those stairs."

"You're really taking me back?"

He nodded. "Maybe they don't hang women, but they lock 'em up for good. And that's where you belong."

"You're a fool, Ben Hawks," she snapped, anger rising. "You get me in front of a jury, I'll get off free and clear. They'll adore me. And a few tears can do wonders."

"Get down those stairs, or I'll throw you down 'em."

Her chin went up. "You're angry because of Brian. Well, he was more man than you'll ever be."

"That why he socked you on the jaw?"

She put a hand to her face and winced at the touch. "Your precious Roxanna did that so she could get away out the window. But Shanks dragged her back by the hair."

Despite his pain, Ben had to smile. His first real smile in years. "She socked you?"

Eyes blazing, Vera spat at him. The wet struck his face. She spat again, missing as he dodged. Something let go inside of him, and as she spun around and walked along the landing, he followed, realizing with overwhelming relief that he was a free man. His bad dream over, he felt wide awake.

As Vera went down the stairs, Ben followed more slowly. Dizzy and conscious of the blood dribbling down the left side of his head, he fought to stay in control. He pressed his hand over the head wound. Thank God Reilly, Hack, the deputies and the Larabee men had the saloon under control.

When Vera reached the bottom of the stairs, Hack's men took her into custody. As they cuffed her hands in front of her, she spat at them and missed.

Ben moved toward the swinging doors and fading sunlight. Roxanna stood there, the shine of her dark eyes and auburn hair dazzling him even as his vision blurred.

A strange man approached Roxanna, and Ben tensed. Belatedly, he recognized the hired gunman named Hatcher. The man wore no sidearm and carried his huge, shiny Mexican spurs. Hatcher handed them to her. "So you won't forget me."

Roxanna took them, with a slightly bewildered smile at the affection in Hatcher's gaze. Ben understood, even as Hatcher backed up and turned away to hide his face. He decided he'd tell her one day what Reilly had told him when he first came to Carmody, that Hatcher meant the spurs as a love token.

As the posse began filing out the door, the wounded Frye and Vera in tow, Roxanna took Ben's his right arm to steady him. He fought another wave of dizziness as she ushered him out the swinging doors. Another half dozen deputies awaited them with horses.

Reilly turned toward the saloon crowd, most of whom had followed them to the swinging doors but stopped short of confronting him. He pulled his badge from under his coat and held it up. "Any man shows his face on the trail out of here is gonna be telling me he's wanted somewhere. So stay put, boys, and count your blessings. Next spring, I'll be here with an army, so I suggest you clear out afore then."

The crowd backed away.

Reilly joined the posse as they prepared to mount. Hack caught the sneering Vera by the waist and tossed her up on one of the spare horses. She grabbed the saddle horn with her bound hands as they put her horse on a lead. Frye managed to mount on his own.

Roxanna handed her new spurs to Hack for safekeeping. Hack shoved them into his saddlebags. Then he turned to help Reilly wrap a red bandanna around Ben's head and get him on his chestnut. Ben could barely handle himself, so they set Roxanna behind him. She put her arms around him and took the reins. Despite his injury, Ben felt pure pleasure at her embrace.

"Will they follow us?" she called to Reilly.

Reilly shook his head. "What's left in there, they got no loyalty to anyone."

They headed east in the sunlight, out of Little Bend and through the rough country toward Carmody, keeping a steady pace until nightfall.

CHAPTER TWENTY-THREE

That night, Reilly's posse with Roxanna, Ben, Hack, and the prisoners camped in a grove of cottonwoods on the west bank of a wide, sparkling stream. They built several campfires and huddled on the damp, muddy ground for warmth against the cold. Hack's men gave Vera and Frye a blanket apiece and sat them down a ways from the rest of the party, keeping them under constant guard.

Sloan patched up Frye's arm, being purposely rough when he tied the prisoner's hands in front of him again. Frye snarled at him, and Sloan snarled back. "That'll teach you to take on the Larabee spread."

Still dazed from the gunshot wound Avery had given him, Ben sat on a slicker and leaned back against a tree while Roxanna cleaned his head wound and tied a fresh red-and-black bandana around it. Then she sat down and held Ben upright with her arm around him. Sloan came over, covered them with more blankets, and built up the fire near them.

"Keep his head up," Sloan told her, then grinned. "I guess that'll teach him to keep *his* head down."

Ben kept his eyes closed. He appreciated Sloan's gruff kindness, including the joke at his expense. Best of all, he liked Roxanna's arm around him. He peeked at her and closed his eyes again. No longer a driven hunter who rode the night sky, Ben Hawks had come home.

He snuggled against her, pretending sleep. Roxanna stroked his face.

"He'll die and good riddance," Vera called from across the fire.

Roxanna leaned forward. Through slitted eyes, Ben saw her hold up the bloody bandanna she'd removed from him. "You shut up or I'll stuff this in your mouth."

Vera fell silent and looked away.

Reilly had his deputies on watch up and down the creek. Others took turns guarding the horses and the prisoners. Content to leave matters in the marshal's hands, Ben knew only one thing at that moment. Being with Roxanna had to be a gift from God. He felt so grateful, he prayed he would be worthy. He wanted to spend his life with her but didn't know how to arrange it.

As the pungent pine crackled and popped, Hack made coffee and Reilly warmed up the beans. Ben listened with his eyes shut as Roxanna told Hack and Reilly what she'd heard at the hideout. "Rossiter killed Laird Kendall, and then Pecos killed Rossiter because they didn't trust him anymore. Vera told me so."

Reilly wanted to know one thing. "So who was the woman in the stagecoach wreck?"

Roxanna shuddered. "She was an actress they tricked into traveling as Lora Bedloe. And you were right. They planned to damage her face, but the wreck did it for them."

"Nice fellows," Reilly grunted.

Ben felt sorry for those who had died on the stage. The rest of it, his love for a nonexistent woman, had all faded away. Now free of the past, he could enjoy Roxanna's arm around him, the crackling fire, and his new friends.

Roxanna kept talking. "Brian Avery was to marry me, then kill us both to take over the ranch, Uncle Hack. Or at least that's what Vera seemed to be telling me."

"What about the express office robbery?" Reilly asked. "Who killed the clerk?"

"I don't know. No one told me that." She paused. "But I felt sorry for Mr. Frye. He gave up everything just to be with *her*."

She shifted around against the hard tree trunk as if making herself more comfortable. Ben shivered, and Reilly moved to draw the blankets more tightly around them. "Honey, you can't sit like that all night," Hack said.

"For as long as it takes," she answered softly.

The night wore on. Reilly piled more brush and wood on the fire. The welcome, tingling scent of pine chased away the chill in the night air. Ben slept upright in Roxanna's arms nearby.

One of the hands came in for coffee. "We don't see nobody trailing us, Marshal. And it's for sure they won't wait around for you to come back in the spring."

Reilly agreed. "I'm counting on that."

As Hack and Reilly spread their bedrolls, they glanced at the prisoners asleep in blankets near a smaller campfire. "I wonder what will happen to the Kendall ranch," Hack said.

"Laird and Vera were not legally wed. So it'll go to the brothers' family in Boston," Reilly answered. "And they'll probably want it sold."

Hack grinned at the sleeping Ben and Roxanna. "I'll buy it. We're gonna need the room."

Carefully, Reilly lowered himself onto his blankets. "Ben Hawks is the best young man I ever met," he said.

"He's like a son to me."

"Me too," Reilly admitted. "And I saw him first."

"There's enough to share," Hack said. "And maybe some grandkids."

They both gazed at Roxanna and Ben. She held him tenderly

even in their sleep, her face against his wet hair. Reilly, suddenly an old softie at the sight, dabbed at his eyes and lay back with a smile.

Come morning with the sun shining through dark, fast-moving clouds, Roxanna awoke, stiff and sore. Hack and Reilly had built up the fire and started breakfast. At the other fires, men were also making coffee and warming up beans, reluctantly feeding the prisoners as well.

Roxanna managed to slip free of the still-sleeping Ben and settle him upright against the tree. She took time to tuck the blankets around him, then got to her feet and joined Hack and Reilly at the fire.

"You must be stiff as a board," Hack said to her.

"Don't tell Ben, but it was kind of nice," she whispered, accepting coffee.

"You're sweet on him," Hack said.

Roxanna blushed as she warmed her hands. "It took a while," she said. "I mean, he's cocky, like a new colt. He's bossy and wants women in their place."

"But he's got guts," Reilly said, "and he's the fastest gun this side of the Mississippi."

"Except he knows it," she said. "Makes him a little too sure of himself."

"But he's won you over," Hack persisted.

"Don't tell him that," she said.

Sloan rode up and swung down from the saddle. "I was up high on the ridge," he said. "No one's following us, but way off, I saw what looked like Apaches, maybe headed for Little Bend. Not in our direction, but it's a worry."

Reilly stood up. "We're getting out of here."

Hack turned to Roxanna. "Honey, you have to wake Ben."

She went and knelt at Ben's side. He seemed about to fall

over, so she grabbed him and held him up. His eyes were open, and he had a big smile on his face. He must've been listening to them the whole time.

"You can get yourself up," she said, hiding her delight at how much better he looked.

Ben sobered, closed his eyes, leaned sideways.

She tried to hold him upright again. He nestled against her. She thought with a smile that he might not be so hard to catch after all.

"Get up, Ben," Hack growled. "Have some breakfast or I'll throw it in the creek."

"I like it right here," Ben said, nuzzling Roxanna.

Hack grimaced. "I thought you were through with women."

"I changed my mind." Ben snuggled closer. She laid her hand on his face. "Fever's broke," he told her.

Hack stood with his hands on his hips, glaring down at Ben. With a silly grin, Ben said, "I'm a wounded man. I can't be moved."

Hack was hiding a grin of his own. "Get up," he said, "or I'll blast your hide. You ain't married yet."

Ben nuzzled Roxanna's neck once more. "I ain't sure I can wait, Hack."

Hack slapped his holster. "Mr. Larabee to you."

"All right, I get the hint." Ben managed to sit up straight, with a grin so big it hurt his face. All these years on the hunt, he'd had no time or need for pleasure, until now.

Roxanna stood up, but remained close. Ben looked up at her. She was so beautiful, it hurt more than his head wound. He felt overwhelmed with his love for her. He took her outstretched hand in his. "How about it, Roxanna?" Ben asked. "You said I was on a fast ride to Boot Hill, but now it seems your Uncle Hack will arrange it. Unless you marry me?"

Her smile, so lovely, warmed him down to his boots. "I always planned to," she said softly.

She knelt, leaned forward, and kissed his dry lips. He felt mighty content as she stroked his rough cheek. Hack put on a big show of disapproval, while Reilly just grinned.

After a few more glorious minutes, she got up to pour a cup of coffee and brought it back for him. Ben thought of his old friend Luke, with his ongoing troop of kids and probably planning another. Luke had been right. Now he could find his own life. With Roxanna Larabee.

"Ten kids," Ben said as she handed him the cup.

She stared. "Ten, are you out of your mind?"

"Got to keep you out of trouble," he said as she beamed.

"Hack, you may as well calm down," Reilly said. "We got a preacher in town. And that's where we're headed."

"As fast as we can," Hack grunted. Then a silly grin spread across his own face. "And maybe it'll be a double wedding. If I'm lucky."

Ben sipped the hot coffee and chuckled. "You can count on it."

Hack beamed and gulped his coffee down, as if in a sudden hurry to return home.

Roxanna fussed over Ben, bringing him more steaming hot coffee and a big plate of beans. A happy man, Ben enjoyed his breakfast, especially when he looked up at her shining eyes. After he'd eaten, she knelt and kissed his cheek just above his growing beard.

"You smell good," he said.

"That's 'cause you smell so bad," she told him with a sweet smile.

As Roxanna moved off to see to her horse, Ben gazed at the crackling fire. He saw only the future with his lovely wife and many children while his feisty mother rode the range with a former outlaw who'd become like a father to Ben.

In fact, with Reilly around, Ben felt he had no shortage of fathers, who one day would be grandfathers. The thought made him feel blessed as a man could be.

He glanced over at Roxanna, so full of life and spirit.

All would be well. All would give thanks.

And never again would Ben Hawks ride the night sky.

ABOUT THE AUTHOR

Western novelist and screenwriter **Lee Martin** grew up on cattle ranches in Northern California. Martin began writing in the third grade and, later in life, sold 43 short stories, before turning to novels with twenty-two books now published. Martin is also a prolific writer of screenplays, mostly Westerns.

Martin's screenplay for *Shadow on the Mesa,* starring Kevin Sorbo, Wes Brown, and Gail O'Grady, was based on Martin's novel of the same title (Five Star Publishing, 2014). The movie was the second-highest-rated and second-most-watched original movie in Hallmark Movie Channel's history when it premiered in 2013. The film also won the prestigious Wrangler Award given by the National Cowboy & Heritage Museum in Oklahoma City for best original TV Western movie.

Martin's most recent novels, *The Grant Conspiracy, The Last Wild Ride,* and *Fury at Cross Creek,* received rave reviews from *True West Magazine* and were based on Martin's screenplays, as is *Fast Ride to Boot Hill.*

Martin recently left the practice of law to write full-time, concentrating on Western screenplays and novels, often converting one to the other.

The employees of Five Star Publishing hope you have enjoyed this book.

Our Five Star novels explore little-known chapters from America's history, stories told from unique perspectives that will entertain a broad range of readers.

Other Five Star books are available at your local library, bookstore, all major book distributors, and directly from Five Star/Gale.

Connect with Five Star Publishing

Visit us on Facebook:
  https://www.facebook.com/FiveStarCengage

Email:
  FiveStar@cengage.com

For information about titles and placing orders:
  (800) 223-1244
  gale.orders@cengage.com

To share your comments, write to us:
  Five Star Publishing
  Attn: Publisher
  10 Water St., Suite 310
  Waterville, ME 04901